INTERFERENCE & INSURGENCY

NOVELLAS OF THE VERDANT STRING

MICHELLE DIENER

ABOUT INTERFERENCE

Interference can go either way . . .

Cepi may be an archaeological wonder, but it's on a countdown to destruction, and while Nyha Bartarli has been persuaded to take her four wards for a final look at the tiny moon, now she's eager to leave. The only problem is, someone has other plans--plans to exploit Nyha and her wards' status as the betrayed orphans of the Verdant String.

As survivors of the destruction of Halatia, and the subsequent disaster that tarnished every remaining planet of the Verdant String's moral code, no one is willing to go in hard and risk Nyha and her wards' lives--something the hostage-takers know very well. What they don't know is that there is an Arkhoran Special Forces team on the moon with them.

Mak Carep knows his team's presence on Cepi is the last flex of Arkhor's muscle before Kalastoni blows its moon to bits. Arkhor has interfered on Cepi since it discovered the ruins four hundred years ago, but sometimes, interference can have unexpected consequences. When Nyha and her four girls are taken hostage, Mak and his team

are the only ones who have any hope of rescuing them, and they're ready and willing to do what Arkhor does best.
     Interfere.

CHAPTER 1

"THE TRANSMISSION CUT OFF." Nyha unhooked the tiny comm set from her ear and laid it down on the console in front of her, her gaze going to Catano.

The comms officer frowned.

"Interference?" Garett turned to Catano as well, his tone more annoyed than concerned.

Nyha knew he was impatient to get back to his job. He hadn't bothered to hide his irritation at being ordered to accompany her to the comm station located at the top of the Cepi ruins. The fact that it seemed the trip was a waste of time obviously hadn't improved his mood.

Catano shook her head. "No reason for interference." She lifted her own comm set and tapped her fingers on the screen in front of her, looking more and more tense as she did so.

Nyha watched her and felt a stir of worry. "I could stay until--"

"No." Garret's tone was harsh.

She and Catano turned to stare at him, and he blinked, as shocked, Nyha thought, as they were at the explosiveness of his response.

"Sorry." He cleared his throat, still shaking his head. "We're on a tight schedule. The Calling have put us all in a difficult position, and there is simply no time."

That was indisputably true. Nyha dipped her head in agreement.

Catano picked up the comm set Nyha had left on the console and did something to it before holding it out to her.

"It may be it just needs to be recalibrated. I've rebooted it. Put it back on, and if that's the problem, you'll be in touch with your retrieval ship as soon as the comm set comes back online."

Nyha took it, slipped it on, and thought Catano seemed a little too focused on her until it was securely in place.

She opened her mouth to ask what was wrong, but Garett put a hand on her arm.

"No time." He squeezed and let go, but she had the sense he wanted to physically jerk her out of her chair and out of the room.

There *was* no time, she conceded again, and nodded, mouthing a thank you to Catano as she left.

The comms officer watched her with a considering expression and then turned back to her screen, her fingers dancing across the black and green in a pattern almost as intricate as the ones carved into the walls around her.

Garett waited for Nyha at the central spiral, jaw tight. He made a sound that might have been exasperation as she stepped up to his side and she felt the familiar spike of annoyance that had been her constant companion since she and the girls had arrived on Cepi.

Their presence was resented here.

Nyha knew it was because the ruins were due to be blown up in less than a week, and she and the girls were obviously in the way, but they *had* been invited.

Garett stepped onto the thin ribbon of the downward spiral, and Nyha followed behind him. She gripped the handle which protruded from the central column with her left hand as it spun them down, and let her right arm swing out, held suspended by the centrifugal force.

Garett glanced at her over his shoulder, his gaze going to her arm, and she watched him fight a sneer. She smiled serenely at him in response, then threw back her head, closed her eyes, and enjoyed the sensation.

She only opened them again when they reached the bottom, and found Garett had his back to her again.

The walk back to the part of the ruin the girls were studying was less than a minute, and she purposely trailed behind Garett, knowing he wouldn't be able to help himself in turning back to hurry her along, while simultaneously refusing to shorten his step.

The result was a strange dance, and while it was petty of her, she had to get her revenge where she could.

When they reached their destination, he went straight to Professor Faro, and as Nyha looked around the room, she had to fight the fury that rose up in her.

The archeological team could at least have tried to be accommodating, but instead . . . they truly were dismantling everything here. Not only that, the girls would have to be blind not to see the annoyance, the side-long glances of irritation, that had become the standard greeting they'd been met with over the last three days.

Since she'd been taken in as a child, Nyha's presence had evoked strong emotion in others. Sometimes it was guilt, sometimes sympathy; most often it was caution--as if she were a ticking bomb they had no clue how to dismantle. The girls were used to it, too, they'd been exposed to it all their lives, although it was her job to make sure they were shielded as much as possible.

Professor Faro would have to be a lot more openly hostile before he made a dent in the thick shell she'd grown over the years, but the fact that he had taken that tack at all, and set the tone for the rest of his team, did not sit well.

"Problem, Professor?" she asked him now as she approached him, keeping her tone even.

"It's just . . . we're clearing this room." The professor met her gaze with a hard one of his own, but whatever he saw on her face made him lower his gaze almost immediately.

"I know." She tipped her head. "That's why we're here. To see it before it's cleared." She looked away from him and nodded to the girls, who'd all stopped and looked toward her when she'd come in.

With a return nod, they went back to lifting their screens to scan pictures, or crouching beside the intricately carved walls and the strange squares scattered around the room.

The professor sighed.

"I know you have a time limit, Professor. We aren't here to get in your way. We're being picked up shortly, anyway. At least, that's what our ship's captain told me before I lost the connection." She remembered the comm set, but didn't touch it. It was silent, so it must still be going through its reboot.

At the news they were leaving, the professor's eyes lit up, and she had to swallow back a cynical laugh.

She laid a hand on his arm. "Tilla will never forget this. The other girls, too, but this has been a way of closure for her that she will treasure forever."

He seemed to deflate a little under her hand, and she let it drop back to her side.

"Of course," he said. "Professor Dasty was the foremost authority on Cepi, and for her daughter to see it before it's destroyed is only right. If only the timing were better, but that hasn't been your fault. Not your fault at all. If it weren't for The Calling . . ." He trailed off, the fury and bitterness in his voice evident before he took a deep breath. "Forgive us if we've seemed a little . . ." He looked down.

"Distracted?" Nyha knew she was being particularly kind with that description.

"Yes. Distracted."

He latched onto the word with alacrity, and she almost regretted being so forgiving. Almost, but not quite--because as she turned away from him, she knew that she had him twisted up in guilt and relief. He'd allow them free reign until they left.

Maybe they could go somewhere without Garett hovering over their shoulder.

Give and take, she told herself. If being gracious bought Tilla the freedom to go wherever she wanted for the short time she had left on the tiny moon, then it was a price she was willing to pay.

"What did you say to him?" Vika fell into step with her as she walked across the room, and Nyha glanced eye to eye with her charge. Of the four girls, only Fran was shorter than she was.

"He's been close to throwing us out a few times since you went to the comm station, but now it looks like he's finally taken the stick out of his butt--"

"Vik." She kept her voice low, tried to keep her expression somber.

Vika grinned, unrepentant.

"Dr. Bartali." Garett was suddenly beside her again, and his tone was that slightly condescending, slightly apologetic one she'd come to truly despise over the last three days.

Nyha caught the edge of Vika's smirk before she turned. "Yes?"

"Any response from your ship?"

She shook her head. "Nothing." She looked at him expectantly, and he flushed under her scrutiny.

"Well, sorry to hear it." He walked away, leaving her frowning after him.

He hadn't seemed that interested in the problem before, and she had difficulty believing he'd suddenly developed an interest now. Unless he thought the loss of comms signaled a delay in their departure.

That would worry him. He hadn't wanted them here.

"You know, Garett was the one who suggested Tilla come?" Vika said quietly in her ear.

"What?" She didn't believe it.

"It's true. Sugal told us." Vik tipped her head in the direction of a member of the archaeological team. "There was apparently a lot of argument about it, and the professor was adamant we'd get in the way, but Garett had already sent a message about it to someone on the administrative council, and they thought it was a great idea."

Nyha highly doubted the whole administrative council thought it was a good idea. If ever there was a confusing mix of ownership claims, Cepi was it. To the point they'd had to set up an administrative council in the first place.

Cepi had been discovered by the Arkhorans when they'd been taking their first, bumbling baby steps into space four hundred years ago. They'd Rediscovered Kalastoni on that mission, and had admitted the Kalastoni into the Verdant String--the last Rediscovery, with Kalastoni being the eighth planet found that was populated by a people who had obviously all originated from the same, mysterious place and settled across the five solar systems that comprised the string of eight green and blue planets.

Even though Cepi was one of Kalastoni's moons, the Arkhorans had hung on to it, charmed and fascinated by the evidence on it of a culture far older and different to their own. The Halatians had muscled in a bit, being further ahead, technologically speaking, than the Arkhorans, but their interest had been purely academic, and the Arkhorans had tolerated their presence.

It had taken the Kalastoni at least a hundred years after that to be in a position to resent the ownership, but they'd also found it very hard to get the Arkhorans to leave--they were the newest, least technically advanced members of the Verdant String, after all.

No doubt the reason for some of the council taking up Garett's suggestion was politically motivated, or merely score-settling. Maybe that's why Garett was so hostile. He'd suggested they come, but that suggestion had damaged his career with the professor, perhaps?

She shrugged. What did it matter now? They were about to leave.

The girls were packed, she'd overseen that herself, and their things were waiting in the docking bay.

Tilla approached her, screen still raised and scanning. "I think we're all done."

There was a happiness, a calm in Tilla's gaze, that made Nyha glad she'd been persuaded to do this, even though, like the professor, she'd thought it was a terrible idea.

"What would you like to do before we leave?"

"Sit in the observatory. The others are happy to come as well."

Nyha brushed Tilla's cheek with her fingertips. "Let's go, then."

Tilla's mother had loved the obs deck. She'd written about it in her journal, and Tilla had gone there every day since they'd arrived on Cepi. It would make a fitting last stop before they left.

"Goodbye, Professor." Nyha waved to him from across the room, but he barely looked up, flapping a hand at her in a distracted way.

She hesitated, caught between good manners and irritation, and then decided to leave it.

As the archeological team kept telling her, they were running out of time. The Kalastoni had promised to blow Cepi up at the end of the week, no exceptions. The fact that The Calling had delayed the removal of the ruin's artifacts by two months with their spurious court application made no difference.

There were four days left before the ruins were gone for good.

"You want to say goodbye to anyone?" she asked the girls, and they shook their heads.

"Already done it," Fran told her. "While we were exploring the room."

That made things much easier. She led the way out, and took them to the spiral, let them laugh and do silly tricks as they were spun upward.

Ju hung on with both hands, jumped and lifted her legs, so the centrifugal force pulled her body horizontal to the central column. The other three were still laughing at her antics by the time they got to the very top.

Ju dropped lightly to her feet and grinned at Nyha over her shoulder. "You should try it next time."

"Maybe I will," Nyha told her. And maybe she would. After the excessively safe and subdued public transport on Arkhor, their adoptive planet, this was a little wild. A little more Halatian.

Then again, Arkhor had had to take her and the girls in because Halatia had been a little too wild.

There were things to be said for safe. But the spiral was just crazy enough to be fun. She and the girls seemed to be the only ones on Cepi who liked it, though.

The tech that made it work was similar to tech that had been used on the planets of the Verdant String for hundreds of years, so it wasn't scientifically interesting, except in its similarity to Verdant String tech.

There was even a theory that their original ancestors, the settlers of the Verdant String planets, had stopped at Cepi when they'd dropped off some of their people at Kalastoni, had seen the spiral, and tried to replicate it, thereby sowing the seeds of theories and experimentation that would eventually help them succeed in doing just that.

Nyha found the idea fascinating, but the truth of the matter was, the rest of Cepi was a mystery, the spiral was not.

Nyha glanced back at it with affection as she followed the girls. She'd miss it--it was hardly ever used in Arkhor anymore.

"That looks like our ship," Vik said as they all stepped out onto the platform, protected from the nothingness of space by most likely the biggest Cepi mystery of all, the artificial gravity and atmosphere that surrounded the entire moon.

Nyha lifted her head and saw the sleek gray pick-up approaching, marveling, as she had every time she'd been out here, at how it seemed as if she could reach out and touch Kalastoni to her left, or Darga, the small ice planet in Kalastoni's solar system, to her right.

It was as if they were standing outside at home on Arkhor, looking up at the night sky, instead of on a tiny moon with no atmosphere.

No one knew what was powering the protective layer on Cepi.

The planets of the Verdant String had their own grav and

atmosphere generators, but Cepi's ran silent and without any visible power source. And the protective layer was completely invisible. The Verdant String technology was only possible with a honeycomb layer around it, and it produced a hazy shimmer. You always knew the layer was above you, while the Cepi tech was silent and clear.

A genuine wonder.

Even more interesting, it was widely speculated that the reason Cepi's orbit had been strangely altered in the last year had something to do with its grav generator. Whether it was failing, or there was something else going on, Cepi was now on a collision course with Kalastoni.

If the planet was going to survive, there was no choice but to blow Cepi into tiny pieces.

"How long have we got before we have to board?" Tilla asked, her head tipped up to watch their pick-up edging in.

Nyha remembered her comm set again, fiddled with it, but it was still dead. "Maybe an hour. It looks like the ship's right on time."

It couldn't come fast enough.

She knew she often held a grudge too easily, a remnant of the unfairness of her childhood, but in this case, she thought she was justified in feeling resentful of the way the scientists had transferred their anger at The Calling onto her and the girls. They'd been handy stand-ins for the cult and its crazy leaders.

Not that the scientists' anger at The Calling was unjustified. The Calling had fought against common sense and pragmatism at every step. They wanted to stop Kalastoni from destroying Cepi, or at least prevent Arkhor and Kalastoni from stripping the ruin of its artifacts.

But eventually, after they'd employed months of delaying tactics, the courts had stood firm against them. The Kalastoni had the right to protect themselves from a moon smashing into their planet.

So goodbye, Cepi.

The Calling's case hadn't even made sense. No matter what, Cepi was going to be destroyed. The only variable was whether or not it took a planet of two billion people with it.

The Kalastoni had insisted on having a two-week window before final impact in case something went wrong, and would have destroyed the ruins months ago if The Calling hadn't held everything up.

Because of that, the scientists had to be happy with whatever time they were given, and they weren't being gracious about it.

At least the courts, when throwing out The Calling's application, had barred them from Cepi while the scientists stripped it bare.

The Calling had annoyed the courts as much as they'd annoyed everyone else.

And now she and the girls could leave the whole festering mess behind them.

The small, sleek pick-up seemed to drift downward like a floss seed on the wind as it came into the final approach, and Nyha was gripped with a need to just go.

But it was customary for the crew to get at least half an hour of off-ship time, and so there was no sense hurrying the girls to the bay yet.

She forced herself to sit on one of the benches and close her eyes, half-listening to the girls as they chatted to each other and took final scans of their surroundings.

She lifted her hands up and released her hair from the high, tight, twist she'd put it in this morning, shaking it out and massaging her scalp.

It felt blissful to have it down.

She usually kept it off her face because the color was less obvious that way, and she'd spent her life living on the razor's edge of refusing to deny her physiological roots, and her need to blend in to her new home.

Tying her long blue hair in a complex twist was probably a poor compromise, but it was the only way she could appease both deeply-held needs.

The girls had never drunk the waters of Halatia, with its minerals that changed the composition of its people's hair follicles, but their mothers had, and their hair was a paler, almost sky blue shade to her darker, brighter color. She could dye it, had been urged to shortly after she entered her teens, but that would have been denying her origins.

She refused.

A sharp, almost painful, spike of sound pierced her ear, and her eyes opened in surprise. The pick-up was out of her line of sight, having docked below the obs deck, and she stood and walked to the edge of the platform.

"Hello?" she said into the comms set, looking down at the smooth dark gray of the ship, neatly connected to the docking bay. "Captain?"

"Who is this?" The voice in her ear was deep and rough.

Nyha frowned. "You aren't Captain Farga."

Captain Farga was a woman, and whoever she was speaking to was most definitely a man.

"No." The man paused. "Who connected you to this channel?"

She opened her mouth to answer, but before she said a word, someone screamed below.

She stepped even closer to the edge and looked down, saw one of the Cepi security guards had fallen to the ground and a man in a dark blue Arkhor space crew uniform was standing over him.

She drew in a sharp breath.

"What is it?" the voice in her ear asked, but she ignored it, her gaze fixed on the scene below.

The security guard squirmed back a little, then tried to pull himself up.

The man in the blue uniform lifted both arms, and she realized there was a weapon in his hands. She called out a warning, but it was too late.

There was an audible buzz, and the guard fell back down and didn't move.

The man in the Arkhor crew suit turned his head, looking straight up at her, and Nyha stared back, eyes wide.

"Tell me what happened," the man talking to her through the comm set demanded again.

"One of the pick-up crew just shot a Cepi security guard." She spoke quietly, voice soft with shock.

"Then I have one word of advice for you," the man said, low and urgent. "Run."

CHAPTER 2

Mak tore off his comm set, held it up and checked the frequency. After a moment of staring at numbers that made no sense, he shoved it back in place, too nervous to miss anything.

"What is it?" Vasouvy asked, but Mak held up a hand, frowning at the sudden silence from his mysterious speaker.

"Can you hear me?" he asked.

"Yes." The voice coming through was husky and breathless. It sounded like she was running. Which was good.

He heard her murmuring, speaking to someone else in urgent tones. Giving orders, it sounded like, and his frown deepened.

"Who's with you?"

She said nothing for a moment, and when she finally did speak, she kept her voice low but insistent. "Look, I'm not saying anything more to you until I know who you are. Catano said she'd recalibrated this comm set so I could speak to the captain of our pick-up, and you're not her."

Things cleared up a little. "Catano did something to your comm set?"

"Yes."

"When?"

More silence. "I told you, I'm not saying anything more--"

There was no way he could tell her he was the captain of an Arkhoran Special Forces team sent to keep watch over Cepi until its destruction, or that Catano was part of that team. Not without knowing who she was. And probably not even then. "My name is Mak. I'm part of Cepi's security forces. Now who are you, and who's with you?"

She was silent again. Thinking about whether to trust him, he guessed.

"If what you described to me is correct, someone just hijacked that pick-up in order to land on Cepi, and I don't think they're there to sightsee the ruins, so make your decision pretty damn fast."

She sucked in a breath at his sharp tone.

"My name is Doctor Nyha Bartali. I'm here with my four charges from Arkhor to visit the ruins."

The Halatians.

He knew who she was. Of course he did, he knew who everyone was on this pitiful excuse for a moon. But he hadn't thought about her and the four girls with her very much. They were clearly no threat, and they were going today.

He'd been assured . . . *assured* . . . that the pick-up vessel was clear when it came through the cordon the courts had ordered around Cepi.

Most of the cordon guards were Kalastoni, but at least some were Arkhoran and perhaps a few others were from other Verdant String planets. They'd been put there by the courts for oversight, but someone had been bought off, or whoever had taken control of the ship was just that good that they could fool an entire unit of Verdant String special operatives.

"Have you found a place to hide?" he asked her, a growing dread in his gut about what was going down.

She didn't answer him. When he repeated the question, the silence was deafening.

"Shit."

"What *is* it?" Vasouvy, his second-in-command, was a bit more insistent this time.

"Listen up, everyone." He lifted his hand, made a come-here gesture with his fingers, and the five members of his team, excluding Catano, who was stuck deep inside whatever nightmare was going down at the ruins, drew closer. They were all Arkhoran. He was glad now he'd insisted on only working with his regular team. None of that Verdant String Cooperation Initiative bullshit.

If they'd had anyone else with them now, they'd all be wondering if there was a traitor in their midst. Probably a Kalastoni would have been okay. It was hardly likely they'd be endangering their own planet, but that left the other five planets of the Verdant String. He was happy no one had forced him to take anyone else on board.

They were nestled down in a camouflaged lookout on one of the three hills which overlooked the ruins. They wore full space gear, although it was of the lightweight, flexible variety, even though Cepi's mysterious gravity and atmosphere generator covered the whole tiny moon. Mak had insisted on taking all precautions.

No one was wearing their helmets, but they all had them at the top of their packs.

Mak knew, because he had the clearance, that the strange fluctuations in Cepi's gravity generator had led to it spinning off course and directly toward Kalastoni.

If they were going to sit here babysitting Cepi until almost the bitter end, they would not die because everyone trusted a problematic grav and enviro generator to keep them alive.

Mak studied the live feed of the ruins playing on the wall in front of him, drawn from the scanners they had pointed at the ancient structures. He crouched down and tried to make out what was happening at the docking bay.

"Zoom in," he said, and Erenn moved to the equipment near the door and suddenly they were looking at a group of blue-clad Arkhoran flight crew, one of whom was dragging a Cepi security guard away by his feet.

There was silence as the team absorbed their change in circumstances.

"They said the pick-up was cleared." Vasouvy's voice had a bitter edge.

"They lied. Or were bribed. Or were simply fooled. That's for some internal investigation to uncover when this is all over." Mak kept his own voice dry.

"What alerted you?"

"Looks like Catano was worried something was up. She hasn't gotten in touch with me, so either she's worried she's being monitored, or her equipment's been tampered with."

"If Catano hasn't been in touch, who were you talking to?" Vasouvy asked.

"Dr. Nyha Bartali."

"The Halatian?" Fren rubbed the bristles on his chin. "How did she get in contact?"

"Catano must have calibrated her comm set to emergency override mode. Whenever the doc speaks, it comes through on my set. The doc told me Catano fiddled with it, and told her it was rebooting and would connect to the captain of her pick-up vessel. I'm guessing Catano was worried her comms were about to be shut down, but gambled that the Halatians might be overlooked. They're hardly a threat."

"Where are the Halatians now?" Goojie had moved forward and was crouched down close to the wall, too. His eyes narrowed as they all watched one of the fake pick-up crew standing in the doorway of the small space craft that had been sent to fetch the doctor and her girls, throwing down weapons to the team below.

"I told them to hide. The last time I tried to talk to Dr. Bartali, she didn't answer me."

"Couldn't?" Yari asked. He'd been leaning against the far wall, arms crossed over his wide chest through the whole debrief.

Mak shrugged. "Most likely."

"You think the insurgents know we're here?" Vasouvy asked.

"No idea." And it was ruining his mood. "Catano obviously suspected they did know, or she wouldn't have set up the Halatian with the comm set. Or she thought someone on the inside suspected her of being a spy. Either way, we'll find out soon enough."

"Are we going to let someone know about this?" Erenn asked. "I'm assuming Catano tried, if it was possible. But just in case she couldn't."

Mak gave a slow nod. "We're not talking to those jokers sitting at the cordon points, though. And any signal we send out to Arkhor is going to take time."

"So we have, what, a day before anyone turns up?" Yari guessed.

"Maybe longer." Mak shrugged. "And for all we know, whoever let that fake crew through told them we're here."

"So what's the plan?" Goojie straightened.

"We make sure they don't find us."

CHAPTER 3

IT WAS impossible to find a good place to hide.

Part of the problem was that Nyha had no idea who she and the girls were hiding from, and what their plans were.

All the hiding in the world wouldn't matter if some zealots were here to blow up Cepi a week early.

But the other, more practical, problem was that there were no doors on any of the rooms in the ruins and most of their interiors had been stripped bare. Even if some of the waist-high carved stones that had been sprinkled throughout the ruins had still been in place, they wouldn't have provided much cover.

"We're screwed," Vik whispered, summing it up succinctly.

Standing with the four girls huddled around her in a room at the far end of the top level, Nyha had to admit she was right.

She'd muted the sound on her comm set so she could concentrate on finding a place to hunker down, but desperate times were at hand.

She switched the sound back on. "Hello, Mak? Are you still there?"

"Where are you?" His voice was a deep, reassuring rumble in her ear.

"On the top floor, in one of the empty rooms," she whispered.

"Are they searching for you?"

"I don't know." But the chances were, of everyone here on Cepi, whoever had hijacked their pick-up vessel would know about her and the girls. It was their ride that had been stolen, after all.

"The best thing you can do is hide in one of the outside chambers in the ruin walls. Use a side exit, get out of the ruins, and I'll come and get you." His voice was still low, but there was an urgency to it now, as if he knew something she didn't.

"We'd have to go down to a lower floor using the central spiral. There's no outside access on this level except the obs deck." And whoever had hijacked the ship would surely have someone watching the spiral. It was everyone's way out.

"If you stay where you are, you're caught for sure." Mak's voice was calm. "There's a side exit on the fifth floor, only two floors down from you. If you can get down there before they come up for you, you could make it."

The idea of sitting here, fatalistically waiting to be rounded up, and either shot like the security guard or imprisoned, did not sit well. This was at least something constructive to do. "Right. Which side is the exit?"

He made a sound of approval, a sort of hum, as if he were a proud parent whose child had done well in a test. She fought down a spike of irritation as she waited for him to speak.

"It's on the opposite side to the docking bay, which is fortunate. Once you're on the fifth floor, go down the corridor, and you'll find a small balcony with no railings. If you look over the edge to the right, you'll see a graduated series of terraces. It should be possible to lower yourselves over the side with only a very short drop to each terrace until you reach the ground."

"I'll let you know when we're down," she said. "I won't speak while we're trying to get out."

He grunted in response, and she had the sense he was running, or doing something strenuous.

She wondered if she'd seen him in the staff canteen. There had been quite a few security guards, and she hadn't known any of them by name. Although the ones she'd seen had all been in Kalastoni uniform, and from his accent, there was no question in her mind Mak was Arkhoran.

She explained the plan to the girls, and was pleased to see the tension in them ease a little at the possibility of escape.

"Absolute silence, all right?"

They nodded. Tilla was holding Fran's hand, and Vik and Ju were standing shoulder to shoulder.

They had come into the world in worse conditions than this, Nyha reminded herself, and they'd had to be strong their whole lives because of that rough start. They would get through this and they wouldn't fall apart.

She led the way back to the central spiral, every sense alert.

She could hear voices below, raised in shouts. The archaeological team had been found, she guessed.

She waited until everyone was standing beside her, and let herself be spun downward.

When she stepped off two floors down, she heard the shouting below had increased, and she winced as someone cried out in pain.

The lights in the rooms and corridors on Cepi were always on--no one had found a way to switch them off--and to her relief the area seemed empty.

When all the girls had stepped off the spiral, she led them to the only corridor she could see, walking quietly and close to the wall. The exit was a small open-air area, a balcony of sorts, jutting out from the ruin like a strange afterthought.

Sure enough, to the right there was a drop of about two standard units to another balcony that looked the same, except it had no access back into the ruin.

"Ju, you're the tallest, you go first. And wait until we're all down there 'til you go down to the next one."

Ju nodded, and swung down easily with her usual athleticism. Vik and Tilla went next.

Nyha was crouched down beside Fran, showing her the best way to reverse down, when she felt the brush of air on her nape that signaled movement behind her.

She turned, heart thundering, and found herself staring at the business end of a laz. She skipped her gaze up, to the large hands holding it, and then higher, to clash with the dark brown eyes of a man in an Arkhor flight crew uniform.

"Quick thinking," he said, nodding down to the girls below. "Very quick thinking." Then he smiled. "But not quick enough."

They were herded down to the docking bay. A woman and four teenagers surrounded by four armed guards.

Nyha wondered at the overkill of it when they arrived in the big loading area to find everyone else from the archaeological and support teams, some forty people in all, held by just six.

"Settle down," the man with brown eyes shouted when a cacophony of voices rose up as soon as they entered the area. "Most of you will be leaving shortly. We're giving the authorities at the cordon permission to bring in a ship that'll take you all, and we'll be ferrying you across to it fifteen at a time in the pick-up."

There was abrupt silence at that, and Nyha wondered if everyone felt the same sense of relief she did.

"What about my artifacts?" Professor Faro called out.

"Your artifacts?" one of the guards sneered. "Ours now."

This was about the artifacts?

Nyha focused on the man who seemed to be the leader here. He looked in control, and completely sane, but no one could take these artifacts, sell them, and not get caught. They were unmistakably from Cepi. There had to be more to it than that.

As she watched him, he leaned in close to one of the women on his crew.

"Who the hell brought in a genuine believer?" he murmured to her. "I thought Cors weeded out the idiots."

"I thought so, too," she murmured back.

Nyha frowned, trying to work it out, when Faro's voice suddenly rose. "You have no right to the stones. No right!"

"Enough." The leader stepped forward, shooting a disgusted look in the direction of the guard who'd started the argument with Faro. "No one says another word."

He turned back, looked Nyha in the eye and pointed at her. "Except for you."

He started walking toward the canteen, and raised an arm, flicking his hand forward. "Bring them."

At his order, the woman he'd spoken to earlier jabbed her laz into Nyha's shoulder.

"Move."

Nyha looked over at the girls, hoping they just meant for her to go, but the other guards were prodding them too, so it looked like they were keeping them together.

She held out a hand and Vik took it, and the others all latched on, so they walked in a row, linked together.

As they passed the archeological team, she caught sight of Faro and Garett standing together. Faro's expression was one of horror, Garett's was stone cold and absolutely without emotion.

Catano had maneuvered herself to the edge of the crowd, and as Nyha passed her she flicked her gaze to Nyha's ear, then rubbed a finger over her lips.

Nyha frowned at her, then she was shoved by the woman and stumbled forward.

Oh, she got it.

Catano wanted her to keep quiet about the comm set. As if she hadn't figured that out for herself.

But it also told her Catano had lied to her.

She hadn't been rebooting the comm set. She'd deliberately set it to the same wavelength as Mak's. Which meant she suspected something was wrong when Captain Farga's transmission had cut off.

Why hadn't she said something?

And why not set her own comm set to connect with Mak's? Why do it to Nyha's?

Because no one here took her seriously.

The answer came swiftly, and hit all the right notes for Nyha. Catano knew Nyha and her girls would be the last group anyone would expect to be in clandestine communications with a security guard.

Although . . . had Mak been scooped up with everyone else?

She was sure he'd been running when they spoke a little earlier, so maybe he'd gotten away.

She hoped, she really hoped, that someone had.

CHAPTER 4

MAK SLIPPED INTO THE LONG, narrow space--more a tunnel than a room--that ran inside the strange circular walls of the ruins. He'd hoped that Dr. Bartali was in here somewhere with her four charges, but it was empty. There were at least five other such places, and he'd sent a member of his team to check each one, although this would have been the closest to the exit she'd been aiming for.

It strengthened his fear that the reason for her current silence was she'd been captured. And now he had the added worry of not knowing, if or when she spoke to him again, whether she was doing it voluntarily or with a laz to her head.

"No one here, Captain." Vasouvy's voice sparked in his ear and broke through his thoughts, and then the others reported in one by one.

"Right, move back to the new position. Erenn, set up the equipment and see if you can access the scanners. I'd like to see what's going on in the ruins."

They murmured assent, and for a moment, left in the quiet, Mak wondered whether he should follow his own order, or sneak into the ruins. Take a look around.

If he was caught it would endanger his whole team, but he wanted to. He really wanted to.

He curbed what he realized with surprise was fury, and made his way silently back to the two large rocks leaning against each other that lay close to the ruins.

It was Vasouvy who'd discovered that the narrow gap between them led to an open space inside. Mak knew he'd never have tried to wriggle in there, 'just to see where it went', and it was, in fact, an effort for him, Yari, Goojie and Fren to get in.

It was worth it, though. Ever since Vasouvy had found it, they'd marked it as their fallback position.

"Captain Carep, what kind of shit storm are you standing in, and why am I having to call you about it, instead of you calling me?"

At the sound of the unfamiliar voice booming down his comm, Mak dropped behind the closest rock. His uniform was in high reflection mode, making him almost completely invisible, but he wasn't going to stand around having a chat in the open.

"Who is this?" He kept his voice low, but his brain was working again, and he realized the hostage-takers were unlikely to contact him for a chat before they took him out.

"Vice-admiral Sinjin, commander of the Cepi cordon." Sinjin's voice was slightly rough and very curt, and while Mak had never met her personally, he knew she had a reputation for straight talk. "Now, what the fuck is going on?"

"Vice-admiral, are you sure this link is secure?" He was dead serious, although he understood she might interpret his question as insubordination. She was Kalastoni, and not part of his direct chain of command, but technically, while on Cepi, he did report to her.

That he and his team were here at all would be galling to her. It was the final muscle flexing of his planet, Arkhor. The Arkhorans had discovered Cepi, and they'd managed to keep a grip on it even as their claim became more and more tenuous.

The Arkhoran insistence on a secret team to keep watch before the Kalastoni made it all go boom was the last, petty power play in a game that had begun back when the Kalastoni were first Rediscovered by Arkhor and embraced into the bosom of the Verdant String, very much the backward hicks of the alliance.

But Sinjin's annoyance at Mak's current placement was the least of his worries.

The problem between them now was trust.

He stayed where he was, making himself as small a target as possible behind his rock. He wasn't going any closer to his team's new hidey-hole until the transmission was over.

"By secure you mean . . .?" Sinjin asked, and he didn't miss the edge to her tone.

"I mean can I be tracked through this signal, or can someone, either part of the cordon or elsewhere, listen in?"

"You think what's happening is an inside job?"

Mak let a beat pass in silence. "When the pick-up came in, I was given an assurance it was cleared. That was obviously a lie. So I have to wonder whose lie. I chose to report directly back to Arkhor, rather than take the risk of speaking to the wrong person amongst your staff."

"You can be sure heads are already rolling over the all-clear that was given to that vessel." The admiral's tone was icy. "So, you're telling me you've informed Arkhor?"

"We have, but with the relays, it'll take hours to reach them. They'll be coming, but it will be a day at least before they arrive."

Sinjin made a sound of disgust, and Mak grinned, because he knew she'd be annoyed at the thought of having to deal with Arkhoran military warships in her own solar system, and he was Arkhoran enough to find that funny.

The fact that Arkhor, and to a lesser extent Halatia, had kept their claws in Cepi for so long, even though it was a minor moon of Kalastoni, was a festering blister on the Verdant String alliance, and had been for at least the last two hundred years.

Now that Halatia was no more, Kalastoni resentment had

focused on Arkhor, and Mak wondered how much of the glee with which some Kalastoni were anticipating the destruction of Cepi wasn't in part a reaction to the fact that they'd never really been able to claim it, despite it being theirs.

"I can assure you, this is a very secure link, so let me get back to my original question. What's going on down there?"

"The pick-up scheduled to fetch Dr. Bartali and her four charges came in on time, but the crew is either dead or imprisoned onboard. My last contact with the main building was that the team who'd taken the vessel had shot at least one security guard and were rounding everyone up."

"Who's your contact?" Sinjin's voice was sharp.

"With respect, given I think there's a breach in the cordon team, I'm not going to tell you." If they didn't know about Catano, it needed to stay that way, and no one would look at the Halatian doctor unless he pointed her out to them.

"We've got contacts in the ruin, too, and none of them have gotten back to us," Sinjin said. "I might have to compel your superiors into telling me who your contact is, so I can find out about my people."

Now that was interesting. Catano had tried to work out if the Kalastoni had anyone on Cepi reporting to the cordon's senior command. She hadn't managed to find anyone, but there obviously were a few.

"If I get the order, then so be it." Mak checked the time, knew his team would be starting to worry that he wasn't back yet. "I have to move. Do you have any information about the hostage-takers that I don't?"

"Will you be cooperating with me from now on?" Sinjin asked.

"I'll cooperate with you directly," Mak agreed. He would need cordon help and he had to trust someone. Unless Sinjin was being offered a massive sum, he couldn't see her being bribed into putting her own planet in danger by delaying Cepi's destruction.

"Good enough," Sinjin said. "Someone calling himself Veld got in touch. He's planning on sending over most of the hostages, more because it'll make life easier for him than because of any compassionate impulse is my guess. And he doesn't need them anyway, he has the perfect hostages in hand."

"Perfect hostages?" Mak asked, wondering who that could be. He'd seen the file on every person at the ruin, and there were no truly high-profile figures here at the moment.

"Dr. Bartali and the four young women with her." Sinjin let that settle for a moment. "If we try to capture any of his people when they hand over the archeological team and their staff, they've threatened to kill one of the girls."

Oh.

Mak wondered how he could have been so blind. So *stupid*.

The doctor and her young charges were Halatian. He'd thought of them all as Halatian since this started, even though the girls at least had never known any planet but Arkhor, but he'd never fully grasped the implications . . . This was truly a shit storm, as Sinjin had said.

If there was one guilt button everyone in the whole Verdant String had, it was the Halatians.

The doc and her girls embodied the most vulnerable, the most tragic, and the most brave of survivors. Orphans of the greatest tragedy in Verdant String history, whose fate had shown both the worst and the best of the Verdant String citizens.

It was memories of the worst, though, that made all Halatians walking reminders of some of the darkest moral choices ever made.

They were, as Sinjin said, the perfect hostages.

Who'd thought it was a good idea to bring them here?

"I see you appreciate the scope of the disaster," Sinjin said into the silence.

"It can't be coincidence, can it?" he asked her softly. "Them being here at just the right time?"

"No." Sinjin's voice was grim. "Someone may think I'd spend my time focusing on more immediate issues, and saving my own backside from recriminations about how this could even have happened, but they would be wrong. I'm going to find out who was behind those girls being at the ruins, and when I do . . ." She drew a deep breath ". . . I'll find who's putting my whole planet at risk."

CHAPTER 5

NYHA WATCHED Veld stride in and out of the canteen, directing the first batch of hostages off Cepi with a smug glee she found false. It was as if he was playing a game, or had studied a few space pirate stories and was throwing himself into the role of the villain.

No one had spoken to or approached her and the girls since they'd been separated from the other hostages, although she could see the archeological team and its support staff through the massive open canteen doors. They stood in small groups, shocked and frightened, and in some cases, furious.

Some of the artifacts had been catalogued and removed weeks ago, but at least half of them still remained, and that was a loss she was sure Professor Faro would not take well.

It was no surprise he was in the first group to be ferried away. If anyone was going to foment dissent, it was Faro.

Garett hadn't been taken, though. Nyha could see him standing mulishly to one side, staring around him with narrowed eyes.

The girls had initially sat in silence, shocked and scared, but with nothing happening they'd started talking softly to each other while Nyha kept watch.

She'd arranged the chairs so they sat behind her in a tight circle, tucked into a corner of the room, and she put herself between them and everyone else.

The canteen was the biggest single room on Cepi--whoever had created the curved buildings with their smooth black surfaces had either been much smaller than the people of the Verdant String, or they'd liked small spaces--but even so, Nyha felt too close to the laz guns and the hard-faced hostage-takers gathered in the room, and needed a barrier between them and the girls.

She wanted to talk to Mak, let him know they'd been taken, but the canteen was too open, and while no one had spoken to them since they'd been moved here, she was under no illusion they weren't being watched.

She tensed, then curled her hands into fists on the table when the young hostage-taker who'd fought with Faro sauntered over to them.

"Boss says you need to join him over there." He pointed to Veld, who'd come back in to the canteen and was setting up a scanner on one of the tables near the doors.

Nyha stood and looked over her shoulder at the girls. "I'll just be--"

"Quiet!" The guard reached out and slapped her, and she turned back to him, jaw slack with surprise, the sting of his handprint on her cheek throbbing in time with her heartbeat.

The crack of sound seemed to act like a switch, plunging the canteen into silence.

He smirked at her, and in his face, just for a moment, she saw the smuggler who had terrorized her on her journey from Halatia to Arkhor fifteen years ago.

It was extraordinary.

She'd spent her life since then, since she was twelve, coming to terms with what had happened to her, to her family, to everyone she knew. The greed and corruption that had led to her being assaulted by a group of criminals, and the moral bankruptcy that had put her in the position in the first place.

She had been saved, she made herself remember. She had been rescued and given a home, and the girls behind her, infants at the time, had been too young to know the terror and the fear of the smuggler ships.

But if they had, they would see this asshole was of the same breed.

A hand landed on the smirker's shoulder, heavy enough to make him wince and dip down on one side.

"What did you just do?" The voice was surprisingly neutral.

Nyha looked up, and her gaze clashed with Veld's.

"Put her in her place." The smirker tried to move to one side, get out of the hold, and winced when it tightened.

"I'm about to get Dr. Bartali here to speak to the cordon officials. I'm going to tell them that if they do as I say, Dr. Bartali and her girls won't be harmed. And now, I'm going to have to do it with a massive red mark on her cheek."

The smirker cried out and buckled, trying to escape downward now that he'd realized escaping to the side was not an option.

"I was only following the creed," he said, voice high and over-loud in the still-silent room.

"The creed?" Veld's voice deepened.

"The ruins are ours to command, and none can naysay us when we stand upon them." He spoke in quick, sharp bursts, breathing hard.

"What's your name?" Veld asked him.

"Hamand." He got it out on a squeak. "It's an honor to be chosen-"

"Cors." Veld interrupted, keeping his grip on Hamand's shoulder, but turning to look behind him. One of the big, older men in the group hunched his shoulders.

"He slipped through."

"Deal with him." Veld pivoted Hamand around and shoved him in Cors' direction.

Cors sighed and moved forward, faster and quieter than Nyha

would have guessed from someone of his size. He grabbed Hamand by the neck and dragged him out the room.

Nyha watched the other members of the group as they avoided Veld's gaze, looking down, or at the retreating backs of Cors and Hamand.

"Are you all right?" Veld turned to her, and she lifted a brow.

"No. If you're concerned about my well-being, let me and the girls go."

Veld smirked, his eyes gleaming with humor. "I'm afraid that isn't possible. Come, I want you to talk to the cordon authorities."

"What do you want me to tell them?"

"The truth." Veld put a hand on her arm and pulled her toward him, but he wasn't rough and his grip was light enough.

"Nyha . . ." Vik's voice wobbled.

Nyha turned, and saw all the girls were out of their seats. There was a readiness about them, the *Kal Maroo* training she'd forced on them over the years apparent in the way they stood, ready to spring.

She gave a tiny shake of her head so they would stand down, and tried to smile. "Sit. It's okay. I'm just going to where they've set up the scanners."

They lowered themselves slowly, and Nyha saw they were all focused on her face.

She brushed her fingertips over her cheek and forced herself not to wince.

"Time's wasting, Dr. Bartali." Veld started walking to the table where his crew had set up the comm equipment.

She followed him, took the seat he held out for her.

"I want them to see your hair." He leaned over her and lifted the hair that hung down her back and flicked it over her shoulders so it hung on either side of her face.

She looked up at him, confused, but he'd turned to watch the pick-up as it lifted up and disappeared into the sky above, carrying away the first set of hostages.

About two thirds of the Cepi staff where still left standing in the docking bay. Of everyone they could have chosen to speak to the authorities, why choose her? Professor Faro would surely have been a better spokesperson. He was known throughout the Verdant String as public interest had focused on Cepi in the months before it was scheduled to be blown up.

She rubbed a lock of her hair between thumb and forefinger, looked down at it, and it came to her.

Anger rose up in her, so hot, so searing, she had to blink away scalding tears of emotion.

They wanted her blue hair tumbling around her. They wanted her to look as Halatian as possible.

They were going to use a fifteen year old tragedy to manipulate the Verdant String into not daring to even attempt a rescue, in case either she or the girls were injured.

She'd had cause over the years to resent some of the baggage attached to her arrival in Arkhor. She was aware of the difficulty some had dealing with Halatians, as the guilt made them uncomfortable and edgy.

But those people were the exception.

Her adopted home wasn't perfect, but it was hers now, and she loved it.

That her personal trauma, and the terrible arrival into the world that the girls behind her had endured, was being used by Veld and his crew for their own purposes burned through any fears and doubts she'd had before.

They would not get away with this. She'd do whatever she could to make sure of it.

"Ready?" Veld asked her.

She looked up at him, trying hard to appear calm.

"I still don't know what you want me to do."

"I'm going to connect to the Cepi cordon battleship. You're going to confirm that you and your girls are our hostages. That is all."

Nyha raised her shoulders. "All right."

But it wasn't. It wasn't all right at all.

CHAPTER 6

ARKHOR SPECIAL FORCES provided top-of-the-line equipment, but Erenn couldn't connect to a single one of the scanners they'd placed in the ruins when they'd first been assigned to Cepi.

"Jamming us. Well, not us specifically. My guess is they have a top-end general jammer. Something cutting edge." Erenn closed down her equipment in disgust.

"So high-end space pirates or smugglers." The way they'd come in, shut the site down with minimum casualties, minimum effort, Mak had thought high-end pro from the start. "Everyone we've seen involved in the takeover so far is Verdant String."

"Might be misdirection." Goojie helped Erenn move her equipment up against the wall, out of the way. "But it makes sense to look close to home first."

"It might be one of the Breakaways," Fren said. "Could be they're a for-profit operation."

"There are only two Breakaways, though." Vasouvy was pacing the small space. "And while they may be all about profit, the Breakaway planets aren't at Verdant String level of tech, not by a long way."

"Not overall, they're not. But a few elites at the very top might have the capacity. That's why they broke away, remember, because they don't like the egalitarian ways of the Verdant String. They want to be able to accumulate as much wealth as they can." Fren leaned back against the wall, ankles and arms crossed.

"Then we have to ask what someone would gain from taking over Cepi before it's destroyed. We know their crew is slick and smart. Using the Halatians is a stroke of genius, but it also tells us something." Mak lowered himself to the floor of their tiny cave, stretched his legs out in front of him.

"What does it tell us?" Yari joined him, leaning back against the rock.

"That whatever they want to do here, they need time and space to do it. This isn't a fast and dirty mission, they need breathing room, that's why they're using the Halatians as hostages. So they'll be left alone for at least a while."

"Good point." Vasouvy was thoughtful. "But then it begs the question, is it just luck that the Halatians are here?"

"Vice-admiral Sinjin and I wondered the same." Mak stretched his neck from side to side, loosening stiff muscles.

"You think the Halatians are in on it? They're kids, aren't they?" Fren sounded shocked.

Mak shook his head. "No. But I think someone made sure they were invited up here and convinced them to come. And I'd like to know who that was."

"An inside job?" Goojie lifted bushy brows.

"Got to be. And not just here on Cepi. Someone on Arkhor, too."

Vasouvy made a strangled sound. "One of *ours*?"

"They used an Arkhor ship to come in, and you can't tell me someone on Arkhor didn't have to approve Dr. Bartali's visit with those girls so close to Cepi being destroyed."

His team were silent as they absorbed that.

"If we're asking this, someone else higher up will ask it, too.

Surely anyone who's involved would know they'd be caught?" Erenn slid down the rock wall and rested her head on her knees.

"Maybe they think they're too clever. Or maybe they've been offered massive wealth on a Breakaway and are about to disappear." Mak let that sink in, too.

Then he pulled himself to his feet. "All right, we need to know what's going on in those ruins. If they've set up a jammer that blocks scanner feed, then we'll have to see for ourselves." He picked up his pack. "Vasouvy, Yari and I will find a way in, and Fren, Goojie and Erenn, you set up at equidistant points just outside the perimeter of the ruins. Erenn, you get the job of relaying our reports to Vice-admiral Sinjin."

They nodded agreement and packed up, pulling on their helmets and leaving the heavier equipment in the cave.

Mak took the lead, slipping through the shadows the strange, reflected light that Burno, Kalastoni's largest moon, cast over the terrain, his uniform set to high reflection mode again.

He would be almost impossible to spot with the naked eye, and heat sensors would also struggle to pick him up.

They reached the closest wall that surrounded the ruin.

If it was a wall at all.

There was a huge gap between it and the other two tall, curved structures that encircled the central building, so it couldn't have been built to keep anyone in or out.

Erenn, Goojie and Fren split off from the back. They'd work their way around to find posts from which they could watch for movement and hold themselves ready in case Mak or his team needed help.

Mak kept moving forward, scanning for any sign of life.

The ground between the wall-like structure and the main building was open and exposed.

He was betting on the hostage-takers having a small, tight crew, with not a lot of spare eyes to watch for infiltration. The pick-up they'd hijacked was small, and there could only be so many of them.

They'd have hostages to watch, some would be ferrying the hostages they were giving up to the cordon authorities, and others would surely be doing whatever it was they had come here to do.

He and his team should be safe.

Time seemed to stretch with every breath, every step, and then his hand touched the wall, and he was pressed up against it, waiting for Vasouvy and Yari.

They hit the wall seconds after him, and then followed as he slid along it and then stopped when he came to the first entrance to the building.

He took a moment to appreciate that there wasn't a single door in the ruins. It made getting in a lot easier.

He crouched, extended his arm, palm out, and curved it around the doorway, using his glove as a mirror. He transmitted the reflection mode image to the inside of his visor.

They were clear.

He carefully stepped in, still in a low crouch.

"Hello, Mak. Are you there?" The whisper in his ear, low and urgent, forced him to put a hand out on the ground to steady himself.

Vasouvy touched his arm in query.

"Bartali just made contact," he whispered. He switched on the comm set. "I'm here."

He thought she sighed with relief. Would she do that if she was being coerced to speak to him?

"I was worried they'd herded you up with the others." Her voice was down to a whisper.

He frowned for a moment, then remembered he'd told her he was part of the security team. She'd probably been wondering which of the hostages was him.

"You didn't ask after me, did you?"

"No." She breathed it out, almost inaudible, and he felt a frisson of . . . something shoot through him.

He forced himself to focus on his surroundings. "Dr. Bartali, can you hold on a few minutes?"

"Nyha," she said. "My name is Nyha, and yes."

He switched the comm to silent. He sensed rather than saw that Yari and Vasouvy were crouched beside him.

"You think she's been compromised?" Yari asked.

"No. I think she's trying to keep her conversation as quiet as she can. Yari, I want you to find a way to see the docking bay, let us all know what's happening there. Vasouvy, go up to the comm station, see if Catano left us any clues, and when you're done, find where they've set up their command center."

"What are you going to do?" Yari stood--Mak couldn't see him, but he sensed the movement.

"I'm going to find one of the hostage-takers to follow and work out what they're up to. And we're all going to look for where they've put the hostages." He stood himself, and waited for the other two to head out before he touched his comm set again. "I'm back. Can you talk?"

There was nothing but silence.

"Nyha?" He moved forward as he spoke, orienting himself.

The whole team had been inside the ruins a few times since they'd first arrived, using it as infiltration practice. The rules were they couldn't get caught, and they had to leave a message for Catano.

Everyone had managed it twice without being noticed, and Mak was glad of it now. They had a good working knowledge of the building.

"Nyha, can you hear me?"

Still nothing.

Mak tried to picture what she looked like. His impression had been that she was slim and short, with blue hair pulled back off her face. He'd been with Erenn in their bunker watching the scanners when she'd arrived for her visit, but he'd been more interested in how the security crew had done their job than in the Halatians at the time. Now he wished he'd paid more attention to her.

He came to the open, central area with its constantly moving spiral that rose up through the full height of the building. It presented him with numerous choices on where to go.

Yari would have gone left, toward the launch bay, and Vasouvy would have headed up to Catano's comm room, so Mak went right, keeping close to the walls.

He heard the footsteps ringing on the strange black stone of the floor long before the hostage-takers turned the corner and made their way past him.

He'd stepped into the shadow thrown by a strange, sharply angled wall which jutted out into the wide passage, and knew he was completely invisible.

There were two guards in the lead, then Nyha and her girls in a tight bunch in the middle, and then two guards behind. They were all armed with laz guns, which were illegal for anyone not in the military. They still wore the dark blue uniforms of the Arkhor flight crew, but over it they wore utility belts with restraints hanging from them, and personal breathers.

The breathers gave him pause.

Was it just a precaution, or did they plan to do something to the atmosphere?

He and his team had their helmets on for full reflective mode invisibility, and they would be fine if something went wrong, but Nyha and her girls, and the other hostages still waiting at the docking bay, would be dead in minutes.

He took a moment to focus on the Halatians. His first proper look at them.

Nyha's rich blue hair was down, and it flowed over her back to just below her shoulder blades. She looked younger than he'd expected; delicate and with a haunting beauty that he associated with magical tales and legends. All golden skin and dark, serious eyes.

She also looked deeply angry.

The girls were calmer than he'd thought they'd be, and also, achingly young. They were a tight unit, holding on to each other as they walked, but in a way that spoke of shared strength, not abject fear.

"In there."

The front two guards, a man and a woman, stopped outside the entrance to a room, and the man pointed inside.

Nyha and the girls edged past them and went inside, and the man pointed a finger at the two guards behind them.

"Keep watch. Don't touch them or talk to them. Understand?"

Mak frowned at the warning, particularly as it seemed focused on the younger of the two men.

Neither of them acknowledged the order.

"I won't be so forgiving the second time around, Hamand, so don't mess up." The burly man jabbed his finger directly at the guard, a snarl in his voice, then turned to the other one. "Baint, I'll hold you just as responsible if he does anything stupid."

The pair gave a reluctant nod.

The woman with the man giving orders muttered something to him under her breath as they walked off, and the younger guard made a face at their backs as they turned a corner and disappeared.

Interesting.

And worrying.

Mak didn't want to leave Nyha and her girls with the guards when even their own people suspected them of being dangerous, but hopefully the warning would hold them for now, and the two clearly senior members of the team weren't going back the way they'd come, but were headed deeper into the building.

He had to follow them.

Mak ghosted past the doorway, looking in as he went by, and saw it was a reasonable-sized room and the girls were huddled in the far corner, with Nyha between them and the guards.

Her cheek looked bruised, and he shot a sharp look at the guard the older, bigger man had called Hamand. Had he hit her?

He memorized the man's face, then forced himself to speed up a little to keep up with the two guards he was following, fighting back a hot surge of anger and trying to replace it with the cold edge of patience.

There would be a reckoning. It was just a matter of when.

The two hostage takers were talking to each other in low voices that echoed in the empty stone structure.

They were Arkhoran, no doubt about it.

Which was not good.

Kalastoni already resented Arkhor for the centuries they'd held on to Cepi. Now some Arkhorans were putting everyone on Kalastoni at risk, and using the Halatians as hostages was just another twisted touch.

Mak would stop them, and he would enjoy every minute of it. These people were trying to drag Arkhor down, make them the pariahs of the Verdant String, and he would *not* allow it.

"Mak, are you there?" The whisper in his ear made him stop. Her voice eased some of the tension he was feeling.

"Yes." He was far enough behind the two senior guards and they were talking loudly enough, he thought it safe to reply. "I'm following two of the hostage-takers who took you to that room. What can you tell me about them?"

There was a moment of startled silence. "You *saw* us? Where were you?"

"Don't worry about that. Do you have any information for me?" He could hear the girls talking in the background, guessed she had her back turned to the door and was pretending to be part of the conversation.

"The man is Cors, and I think he's the operations officer. He was definitely the one who vetted the members of the group, because he was in trouble for letting Hamand slip through. I think they're an offshoot of The Calling, or they're a group who used The Calling as a front. Hamand seems to be a genuine believer, and that's a problem for Veld, the leader. He hasn't got time for ideology."

The Calling. Mak shook his head. This just got stranger and stranger. The Calling wasn't an Arkhoran cult. It was supposedly a Kalastoni movement, but there were a few people from all over the Verdant String who'd joined up.

"The woman is called Garde. She's the second-in-command. I don't know any more about either of them."

"It's more than I had before." Mak shortened his step as Garde and Cors slowed down up ahead. "I'm going to put you on silent for a while. Hang on."

He edged closer. There were plenty of shadows, but even if there hadn't been, it would have been hard for them to spot him.

He stepped carefully into a roughly circular room, one he'd been in before when he'd infiltrated the ruins for fun a while back. He leaned against the wall in a nice deep shadow created by the strange dimensions of the room.

Cors and Garde stood in the center, on either side of a circular carved disk that was flush with the floor. They sunk to their haunches and put their hands on it.

"In three, two, one." Garde counted down, and then moved her hands clockwise, while Cors mirrored her on the other side.

The disk turned, and they stepped back as it seemed to sink into the floor, in a way that didn't make sense.

Its diameter when they'd turned it was more or less the length of Mak's arm, shoulder to wrist, but as it fell away it seemed to take more of the floor with it, as if the ground were liquid, not solid.

"Freaks me out, every time," Cors said, and Mak found himself agreeing with him.

"Come on." Garde dropped into the hole, and after a moment's hesitation, Cors did the same.

Mak walked carefully forward, testing each step, until he reached the edge of the hole.

He couldn't see anything inside it, it was pitch black.

He tapped his comm set to switch to the team's frequency. "Checking in," he said. "I've followed the two senior lieutenants of this op to a strange-as-shit hole in the ground. I'm going to follow them. It's in that circular room we've all been in before, to the right of the entrance. The hostages are in a room down the same passageway. Also, no way in hell they just found this, so it's an inside job. Erenn, tell Sinjin to hold every single member of the Cepi team who is handed over and start questioning them about this. Wish me luck."

He ended the transmission before anyone could respond, because he didn't have time to stand around talking.

Taking a deep breath, he checked his pack, and then he jumped.

CHAPTER 7

NYHA STOOD, stretching out after being hunched over for too long waiting for Mak to talk to her again.

Fear and worry twined together in her chest, because she was sure he would contact her if he could. He was in danger out there, and she didn't want to consider what would happen if he was caught or killed.

When he'd gone silent, she'd felt the loss of his deep, rumbling voice keenly.

Probably too keenly.

He was a lifeline, the only one she had, but she needed to work on a way out of this without him, too. She couldn't depend on being saved.

She'd thought the same fifteen years ago, onboard the *Dru*, the long, rusted smuggler ship that had scooped Nyha and her family up as they were fleeing the wreckage of Halatia, and then tried to blackmail the planets of the Verdant String for their safe delivery.

When the weeks had turned to months, when the food had run out and first her father and then her mother had been murdered because the smugglers couldn't feed them all--the smugglers knew the children would be a better bargaining chip than the adults--she'd sat with the other children and plotted an escape.

They hadn't needed it in the end, and she knew now, looking back with the benefit of age and hindsight, they would not have succeeded if they'd tried.

It had taken the actions of Captain Drake on the Verdant String planet of Parn to break the deadlock.

The smugglers had not been a cohesive group, and they'd taken their human cargo to every planet of the Verdant String.

The suddenness of the catastrophic tectonic plate movements on Halatia--and there were plenty of conspiracy theories about that--meant there hadn't been any Verdant String help available.

The smugglers had reacted quickly, though, scooping up the small Halatian vessels as they escaped the volcanic activity, the earthquakes, and the mayhem.

And then the world had ground to a standstill as Verdant String politicians and leaders argued about whether to give in to blackmail, and whether they had room for those Halatians who'd made it out.

All the while, people died; either murdered, or starved, or from the deadly Fain virus that swept through the ships.

Captain Drake of Parn had defied orders after a journalist had snuck onboard a smuggler ship and transmitted the true horror of the situation. He'd put together an elite team of soldiers and taken the largest ship that circled Parn, freeing the Halatians, killing or arresting all the smugglers.

His actions had a ripple effect, spurring the other Verdant String planets to do the same.

And when it was over, when they saw how few Halatians were left, the finger pointing began.

That was then, though. This was now.

Now Veld and his crew were using that guilt, that deep-seated sense of shame at taking too long to act, to manipulate the Verdant String.

And she wasn't twelve years old anymore.

She was a respected scientist, and the custodian of four girls who had been born in pain and fear on the *Dru*, and whose lives she had been part of ever since.

There would be no bargaining for the lives of her girls, no matter what she'd said to Vice-admiral Sinjin half an hour ago.

She'd stuck to the script Veld had given her in the canteen, reading it woodenly and without any inflection. She refused to be emotive, to beg for help, to do anything but follow the instructions she'd been given.

She turned to look at the guards at the door, but they were facing away, talking quietly to each other. The girls were still talking, too, their chatter, their innocence, giving her more resolve than ever.

"Mak, I hope you're all right," she said quietly.

"Well, this is a surprise."

The sound of his voice made her freeze, made something very close to relief leap in her throat.

"Why is it a surprise?" She lowered herself back in her chair.

"I'm . . . somewhere I thought comms would have difficulty reaching."

"Are you safe?" She wondered where he could be on this tiny rock that he thought comms wouldn't be able to reach, and couldn't think of anywhere.

"I'm safe enough, just worried about how I'll get back. How are things up there?"

Up there? Was he underground?

"Fine. They're leaving us alone." She leaned forward, and surreptitiously looked under her arm at the doorway.

Hamand and Baint were exactly as they'd been before, talking to each other, their backs to the room.

"Did that one called Hamand hit you?"

She hesitated. There was nothing in his voice to suggest he was affected by that, but somehow she thought he was. "Yes. He's the one who's a Calling believer. Veld was furious when he hit me, and Cors took him off to discipline him, although he seems fine, so I'm not sure what was done to him."

"The Calling believes in striking people?"

"Apparently The Calling believes when they're on Cepi, no one can disobey them. Instead of immediately complying with what he told me to do, I turned to reassure the girls."

"And you say Veld was angry that he had managed to get a place on the team?" Mak asked. "As if there was a distinction within the ranks between those who had bought into the beliefs of the cult, and those who were using it?"

"Maybe it's been a hoax from the beginning." Nyha said. "Maybe they were hoping to use the religious undertones to get access to Cepi, and when that didn't work, they delayed the destruction in the courts so they could do exactly what they're doing now, only with the real members of the group, not the cult members they attracted to make themselves look like a believable quasi-religion."

"Hmm." His hum vibrated through her comm. "Maybe."

"One thing doesn't make sense, though." She realized she was the only one in the room talking, and made a gesture with her hands for the girls to start chatting again. "How could they have arranged for us to be here?"

"That's something I'd like to know, too." She heard a rustle, as if Mak was moving. "Is there someone amongst the staff who was involved in inviting you?"

"I was told today that it was Dr. Garett who suggested it. Professor Faro was angry because he didn't want any distractions in the last weeks of clearing the site, but Garett had already sent his idea to the administrative council, and the councillors had agreed to go ahead."

"Dr. Garett." Mak sounded like he was committing the name to memory.

The girls had gone quiet again, and Nyha frowned at them. "Talk," she mouthed.

Vik subtly pointed a finger to her left, and an icy sensation grabbed Nyha by the back of the neck, and trickled down her spine.

"Behind me?" she mouthed.

Vik gave the most infinitesimal nod.

"Nyha? What's going on?" Mak asked. She forced herself to ignore him, lifting finger to set her comm to silent.

She drew in a deep, centering breath. She had to assume it was both guards, and now she was concentrating on the sounds behind her, she sensed they stood on either side of her.

She stood suddenly, shoving her chair back so that it tipped over to the right.

Then she spun, using her elbow to hit the guard to her left--Baint--on the jaw.

As he staggered back, she swept her foot behind his leg and he went down.

She was already moving as he fell, punching him in the groin as he hit the floor and then flipping him on his stomach when he tried to curl in on himself.

She unsnapped the restraints on his belt, and slapped them on him, using the other pair on his ankles.

Behind her, as she'd attacked, she'd heard the girls leap into action on Hamand.

He'd moved backward as the chair fell toward him, that was her last impression of him, but now she looked up, and saw the girls had him down and restrained as well.

Tilla was calmly moving around the room, picking up the two laz guns that had flown from the guards' hands as they'd gone down and putting them in her satchel.

"We need gags," Ju said, and Fran pulled off the headband she wore to keep her springy curls off her face, and handed it over.

Vik bent her arms back under her shirt, fiddled, and then pulled out the strapless bandeau she was wearing, dangling it from two fingers.

Ju grinned and they both went to work, tying the gags. Hamand tried to shout, but Ju smacked the back of his head, bouncing his forehead on the floor, and tied Fran's headband as tight as she could. Baint was still moaning quietly, and didn't put up any resistance.

Then they all stood back and looked at their handiwork.

"I knew, theoretically, we could overpower them, but they had the laz guns." Fran sat down suddenly on a chair.

"They couldn't kill us with the laz guns, because that would mean they couldn't use us." Vik shrugged.

"Yes, but especially this one," Tilla toed Hamand, "didn't care that much about that plan. When he realized you were talking to someone on your comm set, he looked like he wanted to hurt you. So it was a big risk."

Hamand made a sound and Tilla toed him again, a little harder.

"We managed it because they underestimated us, got too close, and thought they had us scared and in their power." Nyha looked down at the two guards with satisfaction. "We used the advantages we were given, and we did an awesome job."

The girls grinned back at her.

"I thought . . ." Fran slowly stood. "I thought all those fighting classes you made us go to were your way of working through what happened to you. I always resented them."

"You're right, they were my way of trying to control what happened to me. But they were also there to make sure, as much as possible, you would never be as helpless as I was." Nyha smiled. "And they worked."

"I'd say." Vik grinned. "So what do we do now?"

Nyha lifted her shoulders to loosen them. Switched her comm set back to talk mode. "Mak, are you there?"

"Nyha, what the hell?"

"We've tied up the guards. Is there somewhere we should go that you can suggest?"

"You've overpowered your guards?" Mak sounded strained.

"Yes."

"Then go back the way you came until the first exit to your left, head out of the building, and I'll get someone on my team to meet you."

"You have a team?" She frowned. All this time, she'd thought he was on his own.

"Do it, Nyha. Now, before anyone comes to check on you."

"All right." His tone put her back up. She knew she sounded snippy, but she felt snippy.

She moved to the door, looked both ways, and then led the girls to their second escape attempt of the day.

CHAPTER 8

MAK LEANED back against the wall and closed his eyes for a moment, trying to get himself under control.

He didn't know what had led to Nyha and the girls fighting with their guards, but given the warnings Cors had issued, he could just imagine.

That they'd managed to come out the winners in that fight surprised him deeply, but he forced himself to put that aside. He switched back to the team frequency. "The Halatians are exiting the ruins where we went in. One or more of you, meet them there, get them to the base, and let Sinjin know when it's done."

"You freed them?" Erenn asked.

"They freed themselves. They're on the move now. Be ready."

He switched back to Nyha, but he didn't say anything, because at last, Cors and Garde were coming back.

He'd been forced to stop following them when the passageway had narrowed to the point where only one person could pass at a time.

He'd been lurking, waiting for them to come back. Which at least meant he'd been able to respond to Nyha, to get things moving for their extraction.

"It's impossible to move it. I don't care what Veld says, there is no way we're getting that thing out of that room." Cors clumped toward him, sounding frustrated.

"Then we have to take it apart, bring it up piece by piece." Garde sounded implacable. "Leaving without it is not an option."

"How can we take it apart when we don't even know how it works? It could blow up on us." Cors passed Mak at a fast clip, his footsteps projecting his anger.

"Better to be blown up trying to get it out than find ourselves without it. That I can promise you. We're in line for big money, but Veld had to contract with some really nasty people for that kind of pay-off." Garde didn't sound worried at all.

"Then everyone comes down here to help," Cors said, tone short and suspicious.

"What's that supposed to mean?"

Their voices faded a little as they got ahead of him, and Mak followed behind them. He needed to know how to get back up before he went down the passageway to see what they'd been doing.

"It means you sound pretty relaxed about the dangers of this place blowing up, so my guess is you and Veld have yourselves a little Plan B, one that doesn't include me, or anyone else on the team."

Garde was quiet for a beat. "You think Veld is going to cheat you?"

"I think Veld, and you, are good at looking after yourselves, and that you'd happily send me and the rest of the team in there to 'dismantle' it and make sure you're high and dry somewhere else in case it does blow."

Mak realized they'd slowed as their argument heated up, and he was almost on top of them.

"Does anyone else think this?" Garde's voice had taken on an edge now.

"No one here is stupid, except maybe for that idiot Hamand."

"Who *you* let in." Garde lifted the light she'd been using to illuminate the way, and it reflected off Cors's face as he loomed over her, all angles and snarling mouth.

"He never said a thing about being a believer when I vetted him." Cors gave a shrug in response. "Look. All I'm saying is I'm not risking my neck for the tiny percentage Veld's promised me, while the two of you sit pretty somewhere else."

Garde seemed to relax. "Fair enough. We'll be down here, helping. I think Veld wants to be personally involved to make sure nothing goes wrong, anyway."

Cors laughed at that. "Like he'd know, one way or the other."

Mak saw Garde stiffen for a moment, and then she relaxed and laughed with him, clapping him on the shoulder.

She walked a few steps to one side, lifting her light again, and Mak saw another circle in the floor.

She crouched down, turning it by herself this time, and the ceiling above suddenly had a hole in it.

Which probably meant after he'd gone down, the hole in the chamber above had closed.

Cors stepped into the middle of the circle and disappeared, and Garde followed.

Mak waited, counting it out, until the light spilling down from above was snuffed out.

Two minutes.

"Nyha, are you and the girls out yet? Cors and Garde are coming your way."

"No." Her whisper was a hiss in his ear. "There were a few of Veld's crew in the central area, so we had to wait for them to leave."

"Go as quickly as you can. They're coming up behind you."

And there was no doubt they'd check in on their hostages on the way past, find Hamand and his friend tied up.

He stood, undecided for a moment, and then crouched down to turn the disk, stepping onto it as a hole opened up above his head.

He blinked and found himself on the edge of the hole in the circular room, and ran as silently as he could out the door.

He could check out whatever was down there later, now he knew where it was. Nyha and the girls, however, needed him right now.

Nyha pointed down the passage that hopefully led out, and made the girls go ahead of her.

She'd told them someone would be meeting them, getting them to safety, and they hadn't asked questions, they'd simply followed her lead.

She was proud of them.

They ran one at a time, keeping close to the wall. Ju was last, and as she started off, Nyha heard a shout behind her.

"Go," she mouthed when Ju turned back, eyes wide. "Go!"

She waited a beat until she was sure Ju had obeyed her, and then she turned and ran toward the central spiral, out into the open.

Distract, that was all she could think of. Distract, and they would waste time getting her while the girls got away.

She heard another shout, more purposeful, and looked to her right.

Cors stood on the other side of the central space. Their gazes clashed, and the rage in his eyes spurred her toward the spiral a little faster.

Two men ran in at the sound of Cors's shout, and Nyha wasted a moment looking in their direction.

She jumped for the spiral, hand out to catch hold of a handle, and was hauled back by a thick-set arm curled around her waist and then swung away from her escape route.

Cors could really move, was all she could think as he shoved her in front of him, and she stumbled in an attempt to keep her balance.

"No." Garde's voice was sharp, a crack of sound that echoed in the atrium, and when Nyha looked back, she saw Cors lowering his arm.

"What's wrong with you?" Garde walked forward, boots ringing with every step. "She's our insurance policy. No touching." Her hand gripped Nyha's arm and pulled her away from Cors. "Have you lost your mind?"

Cors seethed for a moment, and then gave a shrug, the effort of getting his rage under control clearly visible. "Adrenalin."

"Right." Garde eyed him suspiciously. "Go free those idiots you left to guard the Halatians. I'll go after the girls, they can't have gotten far without their leader." She pointed to the two men who'd come to help. "You take this one to Veld, and don't let her out of your sight."

She shoved Nyha at them, then stalked off toward the exit the girls had taken.

Cors gave Nyha a last, vicious look, and strode off himself.

Doesn't like taking orders, Nyha thought.

"Move," one of the men Garde had left her with barked at her, pushing her in the direction of the canteen.

Nyha moved, following the first guard, with the second falling in behind her.

"Nyha, don't react, just keep walking." Mak's whisper in her comm unit made her stumble.

"I'm walking right next to you, but you can't see me. I'm going to grab you by your waist, and I want you to stand on my boots, and I'll press you up against the wall, so I block you with my body. Stay absolutely still, and they won't be able to see either of us. Nod if you've got that."

She nodded, felt the soft brush of a glove on her arm.

Suddenly, the guard behind her cried out in alarm, and two strong hands clamped her waist.

She was lifted up and swung around, pushed up, as he said, against the wall.

She leaned in to him, against an invisible chest, settled her feet on invisible boots, and tried not to breathe.

"Where the fuck is she? What the fuck happened?" the guard at the front shouted.

"Someone hit me on the head from behind, I spun to look and when I turned back she was gone. How did she get past you?"

"She didn't get past me. She must have gotten past you."

She couldn't see them through Mak's bulk, but it sounded like they were standing in place, turning around and around as if she would somehow reappear.

"Shit. How are we going to explain this?"

"Let's search a little longer. How far could she get? You go forward, I'll go back."

They split up, running in the agreed directions.

"Good trick," Nyha whispered.

"Not bad, I'll admit." The answer rumbled down her comm set, even though he was right in front of her, so she guessed he was wearing a helmet. She lifted her hands and patted his face to find out, discovered she was right.

The arms around her tightened for a moment. "My team has your girls. They got them just before Garde came running out. They're safe."

She tipped her head forward, rested it against his chest. "Thank you."

"We can't go out the same way they did, not yet. And my bet is Garde will be coming back any minute."

He sounded like he was sorting through his options.

"What would you be doing if I wasn't with you?" she asked.

"I'd be looking into a strange hole in the ground."

"Want some company?"

He hesitated. "I don't think I have much choice. I can't leave you, and you don't have the equipment to walk out of here unnoticed."

"Then let's go." She straightened away from him.

He sighed, sounding like he had a lot of doubts. "Follow me."

CHAPTER 9

"WHAT DO we tell the girls about the doc, Captain?" Vasouvy's voice was urgent in Mak's ear. "They want to go back in for her."

"I've got her. She's safe, but I can't get her out right now, it isn't clear."

"Right. Erenn's contacted Sinjin. They're sending one of those small pods to fetch them."

"One of you goes with them. Not negotiable." He wasn't trusting those girls to the cordon officials without one of his own team watching out for them.

"Got it. Speak soon." Vasouvy dropped out, and Mak concentrated on getting himself and Nyha back to the circular room.

She stood behind him, pressed up against his back, her arms and legs hidden by his, her forehead pressed between his shoulder blades as they slid along the wall.

The guard he'd smacked in the back of the head ran past them just before they reached the central atrium, and they stood still as he stopped in the middle of the passage, did a turn, as if hoping beyond hope he would somehow discover which way Nyha had gone.

"What is it?" Garde jogged toward him, coming back from the passage the girls had escaped from.

"She disappeared. Just disappeared." The guard rubbed his face in disbelief. "I know it sounds crazy, but one moment she was there, the next, she was gone."

Garde's lips thinned. "Actually, I do believe you."

He seemed to slump with relief at her words.

"Something's going on here. Come with me." She carried on past him, toward the docking bay. "Have you spoken to Cors?"

Her voice faded as she turned a corner, and the guard's response was unintelligible, but it focused Mak's mind.

He'd almost forgotten about Cors.

Mak had passed him on the way to rescue Nyha. He'd been stalking down the passage toward the room where they'd kept Nyha and the girls, fury and temper in every line of him.

Where was he? It didn't take that long to free two people.

Mak hesitated before stepping into the open, central space, and Nyha leaned against him.

It felt good, he forced himself to admit.

"What now?" she whispered.

"We run." He grabbed her hand and stepped into the atrium, keeping to the walls, avoiding the exposed center.

"Slowly now," he told her as they started down the passage where Cors still lurked. "Get behind me again."

They made their way sideways, keeping to the opposite side of the passageway to the room she'd been held in.

When they reached the opening to the room, Mak paused.

Cors was kneeling on the ground beside Hamand, his hand fisted in the guard's shirt.

"I'm telling you, she was talking to someone. Someone other than those girls. We approached her to find out who, and what she was using to communicate, and she attacked. We were taken by surprise."

"He's telling the truth." Baint was sitting with his forehead on his knees, his voice muffled. "One minute they were sitting there, sweet and quiet, the next, they took us down."

Cors stood, held out a hand to Hamand and pulled him to his feet. "Go find Garde, help her get those girls back."

"Yes, sir." There was an undisguised glee in Hamand's tone as he ran off to obey.

"What're you thinking?" Baint asked as Hamand's footsteps faded away.

"Maybe losing those girls isn't such a bad thing."

Cors's response froze Mak in place just as he was about to shuffle on.

"What?" Baint lifted his head, mouth open.

"This whole operation has gone to hell. It was desperate to start with, and there is no fucking way we're getting that generator out of here. No fucking way, whatever alternative reality Veld and Garde are living in."

"But I thought . . ." Baint tailed off. Cleared his throat. "I thought they knew how to get it out."

"Theoretically." Cors's voice was scornful. "I should have known better. I did know better, I was just temporarily blinded by the money."

"Wasn't that high placed official supposed to run inference for us, though? Give us time?"

"With this moon headed straight for Kalastoni? No matter how special those Halatians are, do you really think one high-up can persuade the Verdant String to sacrifice a whole planet for them?" Cors shook his head. "If we had a way to get that engine out quickly, this would have worked. I was just down there, and we don't. No way."

"What do we do, then?" Baint pushed slowly to his feet, and Mak felt a frisson of pride in Nyha when Baint winced as he straightened. She had done some damage there.

"I'm going to have to think about it. But one thing's clear." Cors waited for Baint in the doorway, and by the way the two men reacted to each other, Mak had the sense they were old friends. "We're making a Plan B of our own."

They walked away, and as soon as they were gone, Mak grabbed Nyha's hand and pulled her along to the circular room around the corner.

It was time to find out what was under this ruin.

It was hard following an invisible man, even if he was holding your hand.

Nyha stumbled a few times as she bumped into Mak, but it didn't take long before they were in the circular room she and the girls had spent an hour or so in just the day before.

The air in front of her flickered and then suddenly a massive figure all in black stood in front of her.

His hand came up and touched the side of his helmet, and as the glass retracted, Nyha got her first look at her rescuer.

Steady gray eyes watched her from under dark, straight brows, all set in a sharp-angled face of bronze skin.

She smiled, and his lips quirked up in response.

"Nice to meet you, Mak."

The twitch of his lips turned into a full-blown grin. "Likewise Dr. Bartali."

He crouched, and she realized some of his bulk was his equipment. He had a pack on his back, and he was wearing what must be a space-ready suit.

"Going spacewalking?" she asked, crouching down opposite him.

"I hope not." There was a flash of worry in his eyes, and the light-heartedness that had bubbled up in her fizzled away.

"You think there's a chance this place will go boom while we're still on it?"

He hesitated, and her mouth dropped open.

"You do!"

"It's a possibility. A possibility I'm going to make it my mission to see doesn't come to pass, all right?"

She gave a fervent nod. "I'm behind you on that."

There was that quick quirk of his lips again.

"We have to turn this disk," he told her. "We both turn it clockwise from each side." He put his hands on it, and she copied him, pressed and turned the disk when he did, and then scrambled back as a hole appeared in the floor.

"Jump in," he said to her.

"Are you crazy?"

He shook his head. "Please, Nyha. Just go."

She shot him a look that promised revenge, and jumped.

It was as if she'd blinked and landed somewhere else; a dark, echoing space.

She moved away, knowing he was coming after her, and then he seemed to just be there, in another blink.

"What is this?"

"Damned if I know. But whatever it is, someone here's known about it long enough to set up this whole hijack, as well as The Calling's court application, and your invitation to the ruins."

"Garett," she said, and there was venom and satisfaction in her tone.

"Garett," he agreed. "At least him; probably others."

"Not Faro," she said. "Unless he's an undiscovered great of the acting scene he was genuinely working around the clock to preserve the artifacts, and was equally annoyed with my and the girls' presence here."

"You didn't like Garett?" he asked as he led the way down a dark passageway that seemed to get more and more narrow.

He'd unclipped a light from his belt, but she couldn't see much past the breadth of his shoulders and the bulk of his pack.

"He was a smarmy little asshole," she said. "Hovering over my shoulder half the time, ignoring me the rest. And always with a slightly condescending air about him."

Mak made a humming sound. "You get strange vibes from anyone else?"

"No. Well, except Catano. Who I'm guessing is a colleague of yours?"

He turned and looked back at her. "Yes."

"How many of you are there?"

"Standard Arkhor Special Forces team of seven," he said.

"Ah." She got it now. "Last ditch power grab from the mother planet, right? Arkhor giving the finger to Kalastoni one last time?"

"That's most likely exactly what it was." She could hear the grin in Mak's voice. "But aren't you glad of mother planet interference now?"

He had a point. "Extremely. Arkhor can interfere as often as it likes, if it always turns out to be this useful."

The passage was now only just wide enough to accommodate them single file, and then suddenly Mak stepped aside, and they were in another circular room.

From the direction they'd walked, she guessed they were underneath the atrium, directly beneath the spiral.

"Wow." There was no other word for it.

In the center of the space was an . . . object. Glowing faintly in the same blue as the spiral in the atrium above, it throbbed and twisted in a strange pattern of light.

"Is it just light, or is there something solid under there?" She took a step closer and Mak joined her, crouching down so he was on an eye-level with it.

"There's something under there, but it looks transparent, and then there's a second light source in the center. A tight ball of light."

"This is the grav and atmosphere generator." She circled it, marveling at the size of it.

The generators of the Verdant String would take up all the space in this room four times over, whereas this looked like something she and Mak could pick up between them.

It wasn't precisely her field of science, but the idea that the spiral, which was everyday Verdant String tech, was somehow powering or influencing this grav generator, was beyond intriguing. She yearned to learn more.

"What did Cors say about this? That they can't move it?"

"Yes. I couldn't follow him and Garde in here, it was too risky, but I'm guessing they were trying to pick it up and couldn't."

"How would that even work? Wouldn't it destabilize the moon if they moved it?" She thought about it. "I bet they tried about a year ago, just before The Calling set up shop as a cult."

"Just when Cepi's trajectory suddenly changed," he agreed. "See. It isn't exactly in the center of this disk anymore, it's just slightly to the right."

"How do you think they moved it?" She wouldn't want to touch it, even with protective gear on. It looked too alien. Too strange.

Mak pointed to a pile of equipment in the corner, which looked like it included laser lances as well as simple crowbars.

"My guess is they tried everything they could think of. Nothing worked very well, though. And it's also my guess that they haven't been able to get back in here with the access they need until now."

"They created the problem themselves when they knocked Cepi off its trajectory. And since then, the ruins have been off limits to everyone except the archaeological team."

"They put the whole of Kalastoni at risk." Mak's tone was controlled, but she could hear the anger just under it.

"But why?"

"Greed," Mak said. "Either they want to work out how the generator works and sell the technology to the highest bidder, or they plan to sell the generator to someone who wants the tech themselves."

"A grav generator this small, efficient, and quiet would be literally priceless." And if it was kept in the Verdant String, it would be used for the public good, with profits and expenses shared across the seven planets. Nyha crouched down herself, peered through the blue glow to what lay beneath. "What are we going to do?"

She caught Mak's gaze over the top of it.

"Changing the trajectory of Cepi back to what it was would take months, even if we knew how to do it, and as it's weeks from hitting Kalastoni, there's no time for that, so the moon still has to be destroyed. This is going to be destroyed with it."

"If they'd only told the Verdant String when they found it, Cepi wouldn't even have to be blown up, and we'd have all the time in the world to try and work this out." The *bastards*.

She stood in a quick, fluid movement, unable to stay still in her agitation.

Mak took out a mini-scanner and walked slowly around the generator, then crouched down and went around it on his haunches a second time.

"That's as good a record as it's going to get for the scientists, I'm afraid."

"And now?" She looked over at him, felt her breath catch a little in her throat.

She liked the no nonsense attitude he wore like a comfortable jacket, the dry sense of humor he'd revealed a few times, the sharp, masculine beauty of his face, but most of all, she liked the fact that he was several steps ahead and looked like nothing would stand in his way for long.

"Now we get out of here."

She smiled at him. "That's another thing I can get behind."

"STATUS?" Mak led the way out of the generator room, touching base with his team on the comm set as he walked.

"The pod's about to land. Do we wait for you to bring the doc?" Erenn asked.

Mak stopped, turned to Nyha. "The ship the cordon team have sent to fetch the girls has arrived. Do I ask them to wait for you?"

She shook her head vehemently. "No. Get them off as soon as possible. I can stick with you, right?"

He gave a nod. "You can stick with me."

As long as she wanted.

"Erenn, no waiting. The doc's with me. Get the girls to safety."

"Will do. Fren is going with them. When should we expect you?"

"If we get a clear run, in ten minutes. If not, I'll let you know. What about the other hostages?"

"The last group of them is headed to the cordon battleship for a handover right now. Why?"

"Because," Mak looked back at Nyha, "with me looking out for the doc, and the girls safe, Sinjin could take that pick-up without worrying about casualties."

"What if they catch you? Take the doc back?" Vasouvy broke in on the conversation.

"*If* they get her back, they'll still have just one hostage. They can't kill her until they're done, and they aren't anywhere near done." He watched Nyha's face in the light of his clip-torch as he spoke, saw her nod thoughtfully.

He really liked this woman.

"Erenn, contact Sinjin, tell her to grab those hostages right now, before Veld realizes the full implications of losing the girls and Dr. Bartali. I'm not sure his team has told him they're in the wind yet, but the minute they do, he'll turn that pick-up around so he can keep the last load of hostages as his back-up plan."

"Sinjin's going to love that. She sounds like she'd like to rip Veld's head off with her bare hands," Erenn said. "I'll contact her now."

"Vasouvy and Yari, where are you?"

"Both still in the building," Yari said. "Vasouvy and I just met up on the observation deck."

"Meet us down in the atrium. We're heading there now." He'd feel better with some backup, some more cover for the doc. "Can you make it in five?"

"In five." Vasouvy clicked off.

Nyha had stood watching him quietly throughout his conversation, but as he looked over at her, she grinned. "Better keep me close, partner, I'm going to be in big demand soon by the sounds of it."

"Veld will need you, all right." And he would be damned if the hostage-taker would use her again.

He turned and jogged forward until he reached the exit point.

"I'm going to switch to reflective mode and I'll go up first, just in case there's someone up there." He lifted the light as he spoke, to catch her nod of agreement. Then he touched the keypad on his sleeve, felt the tiny shiver run through his suit as reflective mode kicked in.

He crouched down to turn the disk.

The feeling of being whisked up to the room above was something he'd have to think about. He'd have to try and put it into words for his report, because he knew his superiors and the military scientists would want to know about it in minute detail.

He stepped aside to make room for Nyha and as she blinked into existence beside him, Veld stepped through the open door.

"So, there you are." The leader of the gang sounded unworried, talking to Nyha as if he'd been looking for her at a party and had finally tracked her down. "You've thrown my team into a spin, though." He clicked his tongue in admonishment. "How did you know about the access point?" His eyes were on the hole, his tone was still pleasant, but all of that was belied by the laz in his hand, pointed at Nyha's chest.

Two minutes, Mak remembered. The hole would stay open for two minutes. He started to move, edging around to where Veld stood.

"Garett told me where it was and how to get in," Nyha said with a shrug. "I thought it would be a good place to hide, but when I got down there, I realized it was a dead end and I'd be trapped."

That's right, keep him talking. Mak was impressed at how calm she was, how her gaze on Veld never wavered, as if they were the only two in the room.

Mak rounded behind Veld, aware there was only half a minute left at most.

Veld did him a favor and stepped forward. "Why would Garett tell you anything? Why would he give himself away?"

"Didn't you know?" Nyha lifted a shoulder. "Garett and I are together." She made the word *together* sound so lascivious, even though Mak knew she was lying he felt a twinge of jealousy.

"What?" The exclamation burst from Veld's mouth just as Mak shoved him down the hole.

He shouted as he fell, and it closed almost instantly over his head.

"Where are you?" Nyha reached out both hands.

"Here." He was already at her side. "Good distracting, but let's run, he'll be turning that disk to come back up any second."

She stumbled a little as he pulled her along, and he shortened his steps.

Up ahead he could hear Garde shouting instructions in the central atrium.

"Just find them. Split up and find them *now*."

He smiled. They were beginning to realize they'd lost all their bargaining chips. Beginning to panic.

He liked it.

———

Nyha heard the angry tap of Garde's boots as she stalked toward the circular room, passing the tiny chamber Mak had pulled Nyha into. Nyha held her breath so nothing could give them away.

They waited until Garde was far enough past them, and then Mak grabbed her hand and ran.

She could barely keep up, but they needed as much speed as they could get.

Garde would be running straight back toward them with a spitting mad Veld any moment.

They burst into the empty atrium and Mak pulled her straight toward the passage the girls had escaped from.

"I thought we were meeting some of your team?" She found speaking and breathing difficult as she ran faster than she'd ever run in her life.

"They're here."

Right, because they were all freaking invisible. She was the only one Veld's team would be able see.

"Activity from behind." The deep voice came from somewhere behind her, and when Nyha glanced back, she saw a glittering burst of laz fire that seemed to shoot from out of nowhere.

Mak didn't slow, but although she couldn't see him she sensed him turn and then in a single move he scooped her up into his arms, spun back and kept going.

"What?" It came out as a squeak.

"Body armor," he said. "You don't have any, I do."

She'd seen the pack he had on his back, and it looked like it might weigh more than she did. Now he was carrying her as well and he didn't even sound winded.

And they were going faster than they had before.

Which was embarrassing. She was fit, damn it.

They burst out into the open space between the ruins and the curved walls, and Nyha sensed Mak hunching over her, as if to protect her more.

"Heads up. Incoming vessel." A woman--Vasouvy, Nyha assumed--sounded as if she was right behind them. "Is that a cordon ship?" Vasouvy sounded disbelieving.

Nyha glanced up and her mouth dropped open.

The ship sliding over the horizon was smaller than a Verdant String battleship, but it was still massive. It was a matte black, all strange angles and sleek lines, only visible at all because the swirling white and blue of Kalastoni was directly behind it.

"You responsible for this, Sinjin?" Mak never broke stride. He waited a beat for the answer. "If it's not ours, whose is it?"

"I thought it wasn't Kalastonian. I've never seen anything like it." Yari's deep voice sounded from Mak's other side.

"Where is Sinjin's ship?" Vasouvy asked.

"Coming in at zero degrees," Mak called out.

Nyha twisted in his arms to look left, saw the bigger, bulkier battleship coming in, and then she heard the strangest hum.

"What is that noise?" She looked around, trying to work out where it was coming from.

"They're going to fire!" Mak had never slowed his pace, and they were already breaking clear of the walls that surrounded the ruins.

There was an earsplitting crack, and a hot white light zigzagged down from the black ship and hit the ruins.

The ground buckled under them, and then heaved upward.

Mak stumbled and went down on one knee, holding her closer and tighter.

For a moment there seemed to be no air, and then it came rushing back, blowing her hair around her, sculpting it against Mak's invisible chest and shoulder.

She curled herself tighter, pressing her cheek against the rough fabric of his jacket.

He set her down on the ground. "You all right?" His hands were gentle as they held her face for a moment. "Hang on, I'm getting something from my pack."

She looked back at the ruins and saw the central building had half-collapsed.

Then the terrible humming sound came back.

She put her hands over her ears and turned away with her eyes closed as another crack split the sky.

The world seemed to go silent for a long, drawn-out beat, and then came roaring back.

Something settled around her shoulders, and she opened her eyes to see Mak had draped a large blanket of some kind over her, the fabric thin and nubbly.

"It has some armor protection. Better than nothing," he shouted over the sound of the ruins coming down behind them.

He lifted her up and started to run again, and the pounding boots on either side of them told her Yari and Vasouvy had waited for them, and were flanking them.

"What's Sinjin waiting for? She should blow it out of the sky," Vasouvy muttered, and as she spoke the cordon battleship did just that, shooting a sizzling arc of white at the black ship.

The light danced over its helm, and then it simply reversed away, disappearing in an instant.

"Fast," Yari said. "Never seen anything that fast."

The ruins had fallen in a rumble of sound, but now everything was silent.

Mak slowed, breathing a little harder. He turned to look back.

"They're completely gone," Nyha whispered. And then out of the black rubble, a stream of blue light speared upward.

"What's that?" Vasouvy asked.

"It looks like . . ." Nyha frowned.

"The generator." Mak turned away again. "Run. Erenn, Goojie, get ready for a hard exit."

Hard exit?

Nyha clung to him, looking over an invisible shoulder as the single stream of blue turned into eight or more. The air around her seemed to thin out, and dust whipped up into a storm, stinging her face, forcing her to close her eyes.

"We're losing grav and atmosphere." Mak spoke calmly, and she guessed he was talking to someone on his comm set. "Send hard extraction units. The doc's going to have to share my air, so be quick." He gave a string of coordinates, and then started running even faster through the howling gale that had whipped up an impenetrable sand storm.

She had no choice but to shut her eyes as a massive explosion of bright blue light flashed over them. She pressed her face against Mak's shoulder and held on as Cepi turned into a living hell.

CHAPTER 11

THE EXTRACTION UNITS slammed into the ground up ahead of them, and Mak pushed that little bit harder, forcing his muscles to give everything they had.

His internal suit warnings were sending him minute by minute updates on the deterioration of the atmosphere, and he was hyper-aware of Nyha curled up against his chest, absolutely defenseless against all of it.

She hadn't panicked once.

He'd worried she'd shut down, gone catatonic, but then she'd lifted up her head to watch the generator explode before snuggling into him again.

Erenn and Goojie had already climbed into the cage beneath the bullet-shaped head of their extraction units, their reflective mode switched off so he could see the black of their uniforms through the swirling sand.

He switched his off, too, and saw Yari and Vasouvy had done the same.

He swung into the single seat of the cage, setting Nyha on his lap, and hit the extraction switch. He couldn't wait for the others, the air had degraded to the point of almost nothing.

Nyha was holding onto him with both hands fisted in his jacket, her face upturned to his, her expression tense.

He pulled her closer, hugging her tight, and slid the glass of his helmet open. On his first breath of Cepi's atmosphere, he realized he wasn't a moment too soon.

"We're going to get real friendly, Nyha." He pulled her right in, until her lips touched his chin, and then set his helmet to rescue mode.

Flexiglass slid out from both sides of his helmet, molding itself to his and Nyha's heads together.

As it sealed, he took a careful breath. And relaxed for the first time since the black ship had appeared on the horizon.

"Hold on."

He felt her lips curve against the side of his cheek. "Not much choice here."

He engaged the engine and gripped the cage with one hand, Nyha with the other, as they were thrust upward.

Below them, where the ruins had stood for millennia, was nothing but a crater.

"How would this work if the person you had to rescue was a man as big as you?" Nyha wondered.

Mak snorted. "Not nearly as pleasantly."

"You all good?" Sinjin's voice crackled into his ear. "I think I might have underestimated things when I called this a shit storm."

"Any idea who just destroyed the ruins?" Mak asked her.

"No." The vice-admiral's tone was short. "But I'm standing in the launch bay onboard my ship, waiting for you to tell me every little detail of what the hell happened down there."

"Do you have Dr. Garett in custody? He'll have more idea than anyone." Nyha said.

"That Dr. Bartali?" Sinjin asked. "I'm afraid to say that yes, we did have Garett in a holding cell. A guard found him dead two minutes ago." She drew in a deep breath. "They're snipping all the loose ends, and there is no longer any doubt I have a traitor onboard."

"What now?" he asked.

"Now that we've confirmed there are no survivors on Cepi," Sinjin said, "you're invited to watch a show. Kalastoni is blowing this damned piece of rock to bits."

The massive laser array was primed, but the Kalastoni waited until everyone had landed in the launch bay, and the battleship had moved back to a safe distance, before they engaged.

The vice-admiral was right, it was a show.

Nyha wondered why destruction was sometimes beautiful, and destruction on this scale made it even more spectacular.

"You didn't want to go down there and check things out first?" Nyha asked Sinjin as she stood beside her and Mak on the observation deck. "Recover the bodies of the hostage-takers?"

"The array was in the right position after its last orbit of Kalastoni, and we didn't want to risk anything else happening before we ran out of time. It's our planet on the line."

"I understand that," Nyha said, and then realized there was an uncomfortable silence in the room at her words. She sighed internally, because there was nothing she could say to mitigate the discomfort.

She'd tried smoothing things over for years, and realized it just made things worse. Now she tried not to speak of Halatia's destruction too often, but she refused to keep completely silent because she had a duty, to the girls at least, but also to herself, to keep the memory of what Halatia had been alive, rather than the dead, smoldering wreck it was now.

A hand slid along her shoulder, and then Mak pulled her in under his arm. It was a comforting gesture, but the low zing of attraction that she'd felt since their first back and forth on her comm set roared to life.

The jolt she felt had her looking up at him. His gaze was knowing, as if he'd been waiting for her to catch up.

She sent him a smile and curved her own arm around his back.

"You didn't hear Veld or any of his people say who was behind this?" Sinjin stood with her hands clasped behind her back, a tall, voluptuous, commanding presence with silver hair cut short and standing on end around her face, as if she tugged at it regularly. They watched the laser array reduce the bigger pieces of Cepi to much smaller ones.

"No. The only thing Mak and I heard was Cors say he'd been blinded by the money, which suggests one of the Breakaways was involved." Nyha let her head rest briefly on Mak's shoulder, then straightened up.

"I overheard Garde, Veld's second-in-command, say that the people he'd gone in with were prepared to pay big money, but that if Veld didn't deliver, they'd be better off dead than telling their employers they'd failed." Mak's grip on her shoulder tightened, and then he dropped his arm.

"We've still got the two hostage-takers who were ferrying the hostages on the pick-up, but they seem to be late recruits, they're just muscle and I think they were getting a flat fee, not a share of the big profits." Sinjin blew out a breath. "But we have other avenues."

"Whoever on the administrative council pushed for me and the girls to come up here, for a start." Nyha knew her voice was cold, but she didn't care. Whoever it was had thrown her girls into harms' way for money. They could go down in flames, for all she cared.

"Fenik Darm," Sinjin said. The way she spoke had Nyha turning to look at her.

"Dead?" she asked.

"Dead," Sinjin confirmed.

"They're clearing house." Mak rubbed his chin. "But they either have a far reach, or they've got a Verdant String base."

"Yes." Sinjin flicked him a look. "That ship looked cutting edge, and it was, but we have full-scan capabilities on this battleship and we identified everything on there as Verdant String tech. It's been put together in new and interesting ways, but it's ours."

"Veld must have been able to absolutely sink them if he was taken in and made to talk," Nyha said. "They were prepared to risk you getting a look at their ship, and at their innovations, to silence him."

"Someone on this ship had to have warned them we had the hostages secured and Veld had no leverage left." Sinjin's tone promised a long and thorough hunt for whoever that person was. "The leak is Kalastoni, because until you lot boarded, I had an all Kalastoni crew. Someone here was prepared to put their own planet in jeopardy for money."

There was nothing to say to that, so they all watched the last big chunk of Cepi get turned into fine space dust, and Nyha wondered who had the connections and resources to put together a massive space ship, and fund the theft of a grav generator.

She shook her shoulders to loosen them. Not her problem.

She would, though, put her mind to the relationship between the internal spiral and the grav generator. That they were connected was unquestionable, in her mind. The thought of it excited her.

"I'd better go check on the girls. Thank you for sending a pod for them, Vice-admiral. And for the extraction units. If it wasn't for you, and for Mak and his team, we'd be dead."

"We would never have let that happen," Sinjin told her.

Unsaid was the notion that there were too few Halatians for them to risk losing even one.

"Thank you. And thank you on behalf of the girls."

"Are you their official guardian?" Sinjin asked.

"I am. I lived with them in a group home when I first arrived on Arkhor. I was twelve, and they were babies. We became a family, and when I was old enough, I applied for custody. I'm more of an aunt than a mother."

She looked out at the destruction. "Tilla's mother would have been devastated to see what happened here today. She was the foremost authority on Cepi before she was killed on the *Dru*." She kept her gaze on the debris. "But she would have understood doing anything to save a planet, and she would be grateful for her daughter's safety. So would all the girls' parents."

"Then we've done our job." Sinjin's voice choked a little.

Nyha dipped her head in acknowledgment, sent Mak a last smile, and walked away.

Sometimes she barely remembered the destruction of Halatia. Today conspired to be very much not one of those days.

CHAPTER 12

"DO you believe the theory that our ancestors visited Cepi when they came this way to colonize Kalastoni?" Ju asked as she looked out at the glittering dust that was all that remained of the small moon.

"It's possible." Nyha leaned into her, and hugged her close.

"Do you ever wonder why the ancestors came this way at all?" Fran asked, leaning in herself, and Nyha looped her arm around her, too.

"Given the scarcity of habitable planets as close to each other as the planets of the Verdant String, I'm firmly in the camp that believes they came here specifically because they'd seen the Verdant String from afar. The chances of them stumbling on it accidentally are almost nonexistent."

"But why did they settle all eight planets?" Tilla came up behind them, stretched her arms around them to include herself in the group hug. "There weren't that many of them. They could have all landed on one planet and stayed together."

"They were probably hedging their bets," Nyha said. "They couldn't foresee all the problems they'd encounter on each planet, so they split the armada up into eight, and each took a different planet in the String."

"And all eight thrived. And we all became slightly different, but still the same at the core, and found each other again, hundreds of years later." Ju pressed her forehead against the glass. "Well, until Halatia was ripped apart."

"I'd like to think that there's still another Verdant String planet we haven't found yet." Vik squirmed her way into the group, too. "I'd like to be the one to discover it one day."

"We've discovered plenty of other planets with life, whole other cultures, but never another Verdant String." Tilla shook her head. "We'd have found it if it was out there."

"Well, I'm glad Vik is alive and well and has the chance to look if she wants to." Nyha reached out a hand and stroked the short, pale blue of Vika's hair off her forehead. "You should be proud of how you handled yourselves today."

"Dr. Bartali?"

The little huddle fell apart as Nyha turned toward the door. A Kalastoni soldier stood to attention, her tall, slim frame blocking the entrance.

"Yes?"

"A call for you from Arkhor." The soldier held out a comm device, and Nyha took it with a nod of thanks. "Hello?"

"Nyha? They tell me you're all right. Is that true?"

The voice of Nyha's mentor tumbled and tripped through the comm set.

"Yes, Suk. We're all fine."

"I'm getting reports you were deliberately put in harm's way, and if that's so, HIA will not stop until we know why." Suk's voice quivered with outrage.

"It's okay. I know why. And the person directly responsible is already dead." She moved away as she spoke. The girls didn't need to know all the gory details yet.

"Tell me then. What was it about?"

"They wanted us up here because they knew having us as hostages would result in the softest, most cautious approach by the Verdant String, giving them the time they needed to do what they planned on Cepi."

She kept all outrage out of her voice, all the anger she'd felt herself. Because Suk could not be reasonable about these things.

Suk had been twenty-five when she'd survived the *Dru*; one of the very few adults to do so, and even then, she was barely alive when she'd been rescued. She ran the Halatian Interests Association on Arkhor, and she really wouldn't let this drop if Nyha couldn't persuade her it was already dealt with.

"What did the bastards plan?"

"They'd found the grav and atmosphere generator, and they were trying to steal it."

Suk was silent for a moment, and that was a feat in itself.

"Did they succeed?"

"No. The girls and I got ourselves free, and then the Arkhor special forces team who were already on Cepi protected us and got us out. As soon as the hostage-takers didn't have their prime hostages any more, whoever they were working for blew them up, and then the Kalastoni decided they didn't want any more nasty surprises with so little time left before Cepi crashed into them, so they blew *it* up as soon as we were at a safe distance."

"You saw the destruction of Cepi?" Suk's voice lowered.

"Yes." Nyha kept her voice gentle. "It was hard, but we were safe, and in good hands. And it was momentous. An experience of a lifetime for the girls."

"That's true." Suk sounded thoughtful, and Nyha let herself relax.

"Do you know how we're getting home?" she asked to further distract her.

"Oh! That's why I was officially contacting you. To say Arkhor's vice-admiral says you're going to take the pick-up back. The one that was originally sent for you. And that you're to be escorted by a special forces team."

Nyha realized she was smiling. "That suits me very well."

"You're sure?" Suk sounded suspicious.

"Positive. I've become very fond of that particular Arkhor special forces team."

"All right." Suk hesitated. "I'm glad you're well, Nyha. When the news reached Arkhor that you and the girls had been taken, it was . . . hard."

"The special forces captain was in touch with me from the very start, Suk. He helped us at every turn, and the hostage-takers never even knew he was there. Arkhor looked after us. Their soldiers risked their lives."

Suk breathed out. "Thank you."

That response would have sounded odd to a stranger, but Nyha knew exactly what Suk meant. "They're our people now, Suk. We will never forget, but we have to move on."

"Yes." She took a deep breath. "I'll see you soon."

Nyha said her goodbyes, and the girls offered to return the comm device, giving them an excuse to wander around the Kalastoni battleship a little longer and poke their noses into places they would most likely never have access to again.

Nyha handed the device over with a smile. She walked back to the window and leant against it, looking out at the sight of Kalastoni to the left, the debris of Cepi in the middle, and the small, uninhabitable planet of Darga on the right.

She heard footsteps behind her, and knew from the quiet, light tread who it was.

"I hear we're heading home together," she said to Mak as he settled in beside her. He braced his arm above the window and leaned forward, the only evidence he wasn't completely relaxed the hand fisted on his thigh.

He flicked her a sideways glance. "We are."

"I guess your mission is over, given the rock you were guarding is space dust now."

There was that little quirk of his lips. "True. And the HIA also insisted on protection for you."

Nyha sighed. That sounded like Suk. "It'll be good to get back."

"A warning; they won't just let you disembark like you would have before this happened. You'll be sent to a debrief, I guarantee it. What happened here is not a standard run-in. There are complexities to this that will have everyone in the Admiralty worried."

"Oh." She hadn't thought of that. "Then do me a favor, for every-one's peace of mind; only tell the HIA we've landed when the debrief is over, or there will literally be hell to pay."

"You know who'll be there from the HIA to meet you?" Mak sent her another look. "A friend?"

"Suk Cavada. She was my mentor when I lived in the group home, and she's . . ." Her throat closed up and she had to wait a few moments before she could speak again. "She had it worse on the *Dru* than I did, because she was older."

Nyha glanced up, and saw Mak's hand above his head was fisted now, too.

"She'd studied law on Halatia, and after she was rescued she switched to Arkhoran law instead, worked her way up to president of the Halatian Interests Association. She comes across as strident, but it's just that she'll be worried. This has stirred up memories for her. She'll want to see us straight away, to make sure we're all right. If someone tells her she has to wait, she'll imagine terrible things have happened, and . . . let's just rather avoid the unpleasantness."

"You love her," Mak said.

"I love her." Nyha crossed her arms over her chest. "So let's try to make it easy on all of us."

"I'll arrange it." His voice was gentle. "So, what are your plans when we get home? Got some spare time?"

She turned to him, and just like he had on the main observation deck with Sinjin, the look he sent back was steady and sure, waiting for her to catch up.

She smiled. "Don't worry, I'm keeping pace."

He let out a surprised laugh. "Are you now?"

"You haven't left me behind yet."

He turned to face her fully, leaning against the wall with his shoulder, mirroring her by crossing his arms over his chest. There was heat and promise, and maybe a little impatience, in his eyes. "I don't intend to leave you behind. I want you with me, all the way."

Suddenly serious, she held his gaze. "You mean that."

He gave a curt nod and put out a hand. "Come on, doc. Let's go home."

As she reached out, she had to admit, that sounded pretty good.

INSURGENCY

ABOUT INSURGENCY

The Parnian city of Var is under siege. Buildings are being targeted by insurgents whose only aim seems to be destruction. Nick Bartega is part of the Protection Unit team investigating the explosions, but with no discernible pattern, and no one taking responsibility, he and his colleagues have hit a blank wall.

That is until his neighbor, Tila, is caught up in the first real mistake the insurgents have made. Cornered, forced to take Tila's whole office hostage, the insurgents are surrounded and out of options, until they use Tila as their shield.

Tila sees herself as Parnian first, Halatian second, but her dark blue hair, and the strong emotions her very existence provokes in others means the insurgents see her as the perfect hostage. No one on Parn wants to give the order that might catch her in the crossfire. They'd rather let the insurgents get away.

But Nick, and his commander, Drake, see the first glimpse of a pattern in the insurgents behavior. Not that long ago, Halatians were used as hostages in another incident on the tiny moon of Cepi, and the parallels are hard to ignore. So is this attack on Var an isolated incident, or is there a bigger conspiracy at play?

Whatever the truth, Nick isn't prepared to leave Tila in the insurgents hands. And he's prepared to break any rule, and disregard any order to do it.

CHAPTER 1

AN EXPLOSION REVERBERATED through the cool midday air.

Tila stumbled and went down on one knee, her hand outstretched for balance against the smooth stone of the building she'd been walking past.

Above her, the thin bridge that joined one soaring high-rise to another--part of the City Run--trembled and hummed in the aftershock.

Tila rose back to her feet. She turned and saw the tall mirror building right in the heart of the Hub had a massive hole in its side.

The building was usually invisible, reflecting the city back at itself, so the hole in it appeared as if by magic, hovering mid-air--a crumpled mess of beams and jagged glass, and the inside of what looked like a very ordinary office space.

Up ahead, she saw officers of the City Watch race to assist in their brightly-colored EM vehicles, and then the hum of hovers took her gaze skyward as the Protection Unit flew in from above.

"That's the second explosion in four days."

She turned in surprise, found her colleague, Sarta, standing behind her, her gaze fixed on the damage.

"I wonder if whoever is behind this will finally claim responsibility." Sarta's gaze flicked briefly to her, and then back to the smoking debris.

"Who would want to take responsibility or try to justify that?" Tila gestured at the destruction.

"They'll have some reason. Think of the Faldine War." Sarta pushed her thick, dark hair behind an ear. "I better get going. There'll be no EMs allowed through for hours after this." She didn't move, though. She stood beside Tila and kept looking despite the fact that Tila knew she was right, the electromagnetic vehicles that provided transportation through the city would be banned from coming in or out of the Hub.

She realized her breath was short, that every muscle in her body was tense.

Life could change in the blink of an eye.

She forced her gaze upward, to the Mother and Child, the two moons that orbited Parn almost in complete sync with one another, the Child half the size of the Mother, and always in front, sheltered between the Mother and Parn.

She'd seen them up close and personal fifteen years ago, from the smuggler ship that had brought her to Parn with the idea of extorting a ransom for her and her fellow passengers.

"You get this look on your face when you stare up at the moons," Sarta said. "I've noticed you doing it before. Do they have some special meaning for you?"

Tila froze, surprised that she'd been watched so closely without knowing it. She used to feel the touch of curious, avid eyes like a scrape against her skin when she was younger, when the wrongs and wounds of the Halatian Incident were still raw, but things must have eased off without her realizing it. She'd become used to being like everyone else.

The idea was both shocking, and freeing.

She dragged her gaze away from the sky and turned to Sarta. "When I was brought here, the smugglers would circle around Parn every now and then, to show everyone they were still there, that they weren't going until they were paid, but a lot of the time, they hid in the canyons on the Mother."

The moons were a symbol of her arrival in the place she now considered home.

"If the moons remind you of your ordeal, you can never escape your memories," Sarta said, her voice hushed. "They are always right in front of you."

Tila turned back to the damaged building. "Even if the Mother and Child weren't there, I'd have the memories," she said honestly. "The moons don't remind me only of the bad. They're like a talisman of survival to me. An obstacle overcome. Sometimes, miracles happen."

She was living proof.

Two dead.

Nick stared down at the bodies with pity and a growing anger at the waste of it all.

He crouched beside a woman in her late thirties, her face unmarked except for a fine spray of blood on one cheek, and shared a look with Cris, who knelt opposite him beside the body of a man in his fifties, hair a steel gray.

With a touch of his wand to analyze DNA, Nick had the details of the woman up on the screen that was integrated into the sleeve of his Protection Unit uniform, from inner wrist to halfway to his elbow.

He sent the details to his commander, and then rose as the medical team approached, moving back so they could do their work.

"Four with the last one, two this time." Cris's face was tight and her fists clenched. "I don't understand what whoever is doing this is trying to achieve."

Nick didn't either, but there was obviously something here they weren't seeing. There was no connection between the companies that had been hit that they could find so far. And no discernible pattern in how the bombers were choosing their targets.

Not yet, anyway.

Nick was grimly aware that the more buildings targeted, the more likely a pattern would emerge.

He'd rather they didn't have to rely on more explosions for data.

"To me." The bark of the order from his commander had him turning toward the entrance to the building, and he and the seven other members of his team made their way to Drake, who was standing tall and grim in what had once been a nice reception area.

"It's confirmed," Drake told them as they gathered around him. "Same explosive device as last time, which means it's the same perpetrators." He looked around the group. "Hope none of you made plans, because it's going to be a late one."

CHAPTER 2

THE BUILDING WAS . . . interesting.

And nothing he'd have chosen for himself.

Nick touched the button at the rear of the EM van he'd booked for the day, and while the back door slowly lowered into a ramp, he looked over the ten story apartment building that was about to be his new home.

It looked like a piece of coral growing from a tropical sea bed, all strange towers and pale orange tiles that glittered in the late afternoon light.

He'd been offered new apartments for over a year now, since his inner Hub building had been slated for rehab, and he'd put them off time and time again. He was too busy to move had been his excuse. But that wasn't an excuse Housing had been prepared to accept again, with the rehab commencing in three weeks' time. And so he'd had to take whatever they had for him.

Which was this. Garma's Puzzle.

One of a number of strangely compelling and unusual buildings in the city of Var built by the great Halatian architect, Guan.

Nick started hauling boxes from the back of the van, setting them on the ground, but movement through the trees on the west side of the building had him lifting his head.

A woman exploded from the forest path onto the lawn, looking like she was running for her life, and he swung her way, his body prickling with adrenalin.

She drew up short at the sight of him, jogging in place, her gaze fixed on him warily.

Now she looked calm, but for a moment he'd thought . . .

He shrugged, annoyed with himself, because he'd obviously rattled her as much as she'd rattled him.

He should look away, he told himself. Diffuse the situation.

But he didn't.

She was Halatian. Maybe that explained the automatic protectiveness in him.

Halatians had become an unofficial symbol of Parn's moral high ground, however unstable that ground may be.

Parn had been the first planet in the Verdant String to break ranks and rescue the Halatians from their captivity, their actions spurring the other planets to do the same.

The fact that they'd all left it until it was almost too late was still a mark of dishonor on the Verdant String's collective psyche, and Nick wondered suddenly how it must feel to be Halatian, and have to deal with both the protectiveness and the guilt their very existence must provoke.

He was still staring at her, he realized, their gazes locked, but before he could look away she broke first, reluctantly shifting her gaze to look over her shoulder at the sound of someone else coming down the path.

He could understand her instinct to keep him in sight.

He had no illusions about how he looked.

He was big.

Broad in the shoulder, and after five years on the Protection Unit he was in excellent physical shape. His stocky frame made him look even bulkier and when he was in the all-black uniform of the Unit, he knew he looked intimidating. At least today, in his casual pants and shirt, he looked about as approachable as he was going to get.

The woman was still looking behind her, still jogging in place, although her movements were slowing. She was wearing soft, loose shorts and a baggy shirt. Her hair, the marker that outed her as Halatian, was blue, so dark it almost seemed black except where it caught the afternoon sun, and then it shone a deep sapphire. It was long and straight, pulled back in a thick tail over her shoulder.

He saw movement on the path and a second woman, not Halatian, joined her.

They spoke quietly, looking his way, and then set off at an angle so they disappeared around the back of the building.

The mystery woman didn't look back, and at that moment another EM van pulled up on the rail next to his, and most of his team, come to help him move in, piled out.

Even so, he watched her until she disappeared.

CHAPTER 3

WHILE NICK'S team *had* come to help him, now that most of the boxes had been carried up and the food he'd ordered in had arrived, he realized there was no moving them, even though there were at least two boxes still in the lobby below.

He stepped out of his apartment into the small hall which had only two doors, his own and his neighbor's, and turned the sharp corner that was part of the building's design. The passage kinked and twisted, and was filled with a strange light created by the glossy surfaces on the walls and the angles of the windows reflecting the setting sun off the pale orange tiles.

It was not a sensible building. Not even close.

He wished now that he'd agreed to move sooner. Maybe then they'd have found him something a little less . . . whimsical.

From the outside it looked strangely organic, and within . . . well, he had to admit the finishes were exceptional and his apartment, with its two floors consisting of kitchen, lounge, dining room and beautiful deep balcony, and then bedroom, bathroom and study above, was more luxurious than anything he'd anticipated.

His apartment was in one of only nine little towers coming off the main trunk of the building, each containing two double-story apartments. The flourish with which the administrator had flicked over the paperwork in a screen swop told Nick that as far as Housing was concerned, they'd delivered in spades.

He arrived at the lift, and saw it was already on its way up.

He thought through who on the Protection Unit team wasn't already in his apartment having a good time and couldn't think of anyone except the commander.

He couldn't remember if he'd even told Drake he was moving today.

The commander kept a good deal of space between himself and his subordinates, something that Nick mostly appreciated, and he didn't think Drake would come, even if Nick had mentioned it.

The doors slid open, and instead of his commanding officer, he saw the woman from the woods, her back to him, bent over, trying to wrestle the last two of his boxes out of the lift.

She was still in her running gear.

It was loose enough to hide most of her body, except her long, bare legs.

She muttered something vicious under her breath when the boxes wouldn't move, and forcing himself to do something other than stare, Nick stepped forward and put a hand on her shoulder.

"I'll do that."

She went absolutely still under his hand and then twisted to look at him. The glare she sent him was like a physical blow.

"Sorry. Sorry." He stepped back, hands up, heart sinking. "I didn't mean to frighten you. Again. Those are my boxes you've kindly brought up."

She stared at him for a long, silent moment.

She had warm copper skin, something he hadn't fully appreciated from earlier, which was offset by the swathe of dark blue hair.

"I'm Nick Bartega." He tried to make himself look as non-threatening as possible.

The woman blew out a breath, and he realized she'd been

holding it.

She straightened, tugging her shirt down so it swirled around her hips, and tucked a stray strand of hair behind her ear.

The lift was a cylinder, and its curved door started to slide closed. They both leaned forward to keep it open and their hands touched.

She pulled hers back, forming a fist.

She still hadn't said a word.

"I'm really sorry. I should have realized you didn't know I was there."

She took another, calmer, breath. "You gave me a fright, but it wasn't your fault." Her voice was slightly husky, and he felt a frisson of excitement run down his spine.

She started to edge out of the lift and he shuffled back to give her room. "I saw your boxes below and Fari and Jo helped me get them in the lift, but I don't think I can get them out."

"I was just going down for them. Thanks for saving me the trip." He wondered if either Fari or Jo was the woman she'd been running with earlier.

She stepped even further away, and for something to do, and to make himself look less dangerous, he grabbed the first box, set it down, and then went back for the second.

She seemed thoughtful when he turned back to her.

"Well, welcome to the building." She gave him a small smile and started walking backward down the passage. "I'm sure you'll love it here."

She turned away, and that spurred him into action. He didn't want to let her out of his sight just yet.

He picked up a box and followed her, and when she heard him behind her, manners forced her to slow down.

"Are you my neighbor?"

She gave a nod. "Tila Dor Ria."

They arrived in the tiny hall, and Nick winced at the noise coming from behind the closed door of his place.

"Sorry, I'm with the Protection Unit, and my team came to help me move. They can be a bit rowdy."

She had initially looked at his door as if it might contain the monsters from the Seven Pits behind it, but at the words Protection Unit, she loosened her shoulders and met his gaze with a frankness he found deeply intriguing.

"Well, I'll leave you to it. Welcome again." She turned, but softened the dismissal by smiling over her shoulder as she swiped her finger through the activated laser lock.

"You're welcome to join us." He knew she'd say no, the horror on her face at the noise told him there was no way she'd submit to being in such a loud crowd, but he wanted to make the offer anyway.

She shook her head, and there was something very definite about the movement. He'd guessed right. She would not be persuaded.

The sound of a glass breaking behind the door made her flinch, and he flinched with her.

Not because he cared about the glass, but because he was sure it was reinforcing her attitude that they had no common ground.

The smash had one benefit. The noise level dropped, and Nick thought his team probably realized they had gotten a little out of control.

"We've had a tough week," he said, not sure why he was defending the idiots, but wanting her to understand. "Two explosions in the city. Six lives lost."

She had opened her door and was standing at an angle, so he couldn't see into her apartment. "I was in the street near the second explosion." Something in her stance softened. "I hope you find them. Stop them."

He nodded.

"Well, goodbye Officer Bartega."

"Nick." He leaned against her doorjamb, box balanced on his hip.

She narrowed her eyes at his pushiness.

He moved back. "Please, call me Nick."

"Nick," she said after a long beat. Then she shut the door in his face.

<h1 style="text-align:center">CHAPTER 4</h1>

TILA DIDN'T KNOW how much longer the party next door lasted, but when she saw the storm clouds gathering and pulled back the folding doors that led onto her balcony, it was quiet.

If felt strange to have a new neighbor.

The previous one had done nothing but create unhappiness in the block, complaining and stirring up ill-feeling.

It was enough for Housing to finally move him to a new building, and everyone, but most of all Tila, had heaved a sigh of relief to see the back of him.

And now she had Sergeant Nick Bartega of the Protection Unit. She'd looked him up, found out his rank.

She settled into one of the two big, comfortable armchairs she had set outside. She lifted her feet onto the matching footstool, gripped her mug of jah in both hands, and watched the sky darken from purple to black and the clouds build up until they stretched unthinkably high.

The first zip of lightning set something fizzing inside her. She couldn't help smiling. She burrowed even deeper into her seat, feeling happy, safe, and alive.

She could watch a storm anywhere, she knew, but somehow, here in her apartment high up in Garma's Puzzle, it felt as if she was part of it.

She waited until things started to get really wild, when the wind was howling and the rain started to fall, and then got up and walked to the balcony's waist-high wall. She rested her elbows on it, leaning out to catch some of the raindrops on her face.

A small sound--how she heard it over the roar of the storm she didn't know--made her turn her head to the right.

Nick Bartega was leaning out just as she was, his gaze fixed on her.

She felt a jolt, like she'd been hit by one of the forks of lightning giving a blinding show above.

He nodded to her and she forced herself to nod back, and then he turned his attention back to the storm, and with relief, so did she.

She let herself become absorbed in it like she usually did, and when it moved off into the distance and faded away she sensed him draw back.

When she looked over, he was gone.

She walked into her apartment, closed the doors, and made her way up to the shower, wondering what complications Nick Bartega was going to cause her.

Because beside the fact that his hard, fierce face, and his hard, starkly defined body set her heart racing, he was with the Protection Unit.

She was automatically predisposed to like anyone who worked for the unit headed by the man who'd saved her life.

Not that the Protection Unit was comprised of saints.

She followed every report about them, and she knew they had their small percentage of poor decision-makers and rude employees, like anyone else.

It didn't matter.

The captain who'd saved her had moved from special forces to command the Var Protection Unit, and she respected it for that alone.

He'd acted when his own superiors were prevaricating, using the information the investigative journalist Darline Xan had risked her life to get when she'd managed to find a way onboard the *Caliope*, the smuggler ship Tila was being held on, to send back footage of the conditions onboard.

Drake had infiltrated the ship with his teams, taking it over in a fierce fight that left two of his officers dead. His actions had sparked a change in tactics when dealing with the smugglers from every special forces team on every planet in the Verdant String.

Within a week, every smuggler ship had been taken.

Captain Drake had rescued her personally, scooping her up from the tiny cell she'd been shut in, carrying her through the ship, his body bending over hers again and again to protect her from laz fire.

He'd been a hero to many, but it felt very personal to her. He'd liberated her, and by his actions, every Halatian on every smuggler ship in the Verdant String, ending one of the most shameful and disturbing episodes in Verdant String history.

The fallout, though . . . that was still being felt.

A recent incident where Halatians were taken hostage on the tiny moon of Cepi had brought home how Halatians still occupied a special place in Verdant String society. One wrapped tight in strings of guilt, shame and protectiveness.

As Tila dried herself off, rubbing at her hair, she recalled the way Nick Bartega had picked up the boxes she, Fari and Jo had literally had to push and shove into the lift as a team, all three of them out of breath by the time they were done.

Nick had lifted them up, one by one, as if they weighed nothing.

It had shocked her, and it had flicked a switch inside her. She'd felt a sudden, sharp stab of lust.

That had just been stoked even higher when it was clear he was desperate to put her at ease, to make it up to her for scaring her half to death.

She got into bed, picked her screen off her bedside table, and flicked it on.

More news about the blasts from this last week. Speculation on who could be behind it, interviews with authorities about the victims.

The media weren't allowed to give details about victims or their families, no matter what the circumstances, but she knew how those left behind were feeling.

She'd lost so many.

After a short introduction by an announcer, Drake, the man she always thought of as her commander, appeared on the screen, speaking about the Protection Unit's frustration at having every lead come to nothing and their determination to bring the perpetrators to justice.

He'd been fifteen years younger when he'd rescued her, and the years had been kind to him. He looked older, of course, but he still exuded the strength and purpose she remembered from one of the most conflicted days of her life.

She wished she could have spoken to him again . . . she shook her head, sharply. No use crying about it now. It was all too late, and he had likely long forgotten her.

A deep rumble from outside made her switch off the screen to hear better, and when a second rumble came, she put her extra pillows on the floor and snuggled under the covers, happy the storm had swung back around.

She went to sleep to the sound of the wind buffeting the windows of her bedroom, and wondered how Nick Bartega was enjoying his first night in Garma's Puzzle.

CHAPTER 5

WHEN NICK HAD LOOKED up at Garma's Puzzle the day he'd moved in, he'd only seen the glittering orange of its wall cladding, the strange, organic shape of its main column, and the whimsy of the towers that seemed to grow out of it. Living in it for a week, through storms and quiet nights, had given him a new appreciation.

He liked it.

He ran along the forest path toward his new home, catching glimpses of it through the trees.

One of the reasons he'd been so reluctant to move from his old place, over and above the hassle of relocating, was the City Run. It had been a speed track, endurance track, and obstacle course in one, the high level walkways and bridges between the inner city buildings shifting every day to form a new circuit.

The program that kept it changing still hadn't come full circle to start back at the first route again, or so he'd heard. There were so many iterations, it was still working through them.

But exhilarating as the City Run had been, the forest that was part of the Inner Park was just as energizing.

He'd looked across at it from the high walkways of the City Run, but he'd never thought of it as a place to train.

He'd been wrong.

The storm the night he'd moved in had ripped branches from trees and taken one tree down completely. He'd had to pay attention as he plotted his route.

He'd pushed himself, thrilling at the feeling of things growing around him, the drip of water from leaves and the soft thud of his footfalls on the path, so that he was sweating, feeling all his muscles burn, when he rounded the last corner and found himself barreling toward his new neighbor.

She was walking ahead of him, lost in her own world, until she heard him coming and looked over her shoulder. Her mouth formed a delicate O of shock as he bore down on her.

He managed at the last moment to angle past her, slowing as he went, and stopped a few meters ahead of her. He leaned over and blew out a breath.

"You move fast." Her voice was steady as she joined him. She was wearing her running gear and wisps of her hair had sprung free of their clasp.

She glanced over at him, and then away.

He'd begun to suspect she was avoiding him this last week. The few times he'd caught sight of her, she'd been polite but in a hurry, and they hadn't seen each other over the wall between their balconies again.

Now they were walking side by side, stuck with each other all the way back to their hallway.

He grinned.

"Plenty of damage in the forest this morning." She glanced at him, frowning a little.

There was something so adorably serious about her as she tried to be polite and make conversation to fill the silence. He felt a surge of protective affection for her.

"Yes. I saw a lot of branches down."

"I'll let Fost know," she said, and he nodded, even though he had no idea who Fost was.

They entered the building through the side entrance closest to their tower. The stairs were right next to the lift, and when they reached them, she hesitated.

"My guess is you're going to take the stairs," she said. She gave a nod of goodbye. "Have a good day."

The circular lift door pivoted opened, and she stepped inside.

"Wait."

He didn't know why, but he put his hand over the door to prevent it revolving closed.

"Would you usually have taken the stairs?"

She hesitated. Nodded.

Something eased in him that she didn't try a polite lie.

"Why won't you take them with me?"

Her eyes were dark and intense as she considered him. "Because I feel a . . . tension around you. And I'd prefer not to deal with it for seven floors worth of stairs." Then she leaned forward, pushed his hand away, and settled back against the far wall of the lift as the door rotated closed, her gaze on him unwavering and watchful.

He knew trying to beat the lift was futile, but he pushed himself so hard he was shuddering by the time he reached their hallway.

He raised his hand to knock on her door, and then decided she was probably in the shower, and it wouldn't hurt if he cleaned up before he spoke to her again, anyway.

He ignored the mess of his apartment, the half-unpacked boxes he'd had no time or inclination to deal with, and was showered and dressed in fifteen minutes.

As he stepped out into the hall, he realized the tight feeling in his chest, the thunder of his heart, was nerves.

He froze.

His job was dealing with danger, and yet knocking on a door was making his hands shake?

He'd never backed down from a challenge, and he wouldn't now. He straightened, gave a light knock.

Tila Dor Ria opened the door barefoot, in a pink pleated shirt and slim gray trousers. She held a cup of jah in her hand.

The scent of freshly baked marsalos enveloped him like a hug from his grandmother's kitchen, and he felt some of the tension slip away.

He also found he had no voice.

She tilted her head, watching him solemnly. He could see she was thinking hard, as if her next move would have major implications for her.

"I was rude to you before. Why are you here?"

"Not rude. Honest." His voice sounded rusty and he cleared his throat. "I want to know one thing. Why are you afraid of a little tension?"

She leaned against the door frame. "Does it matter?"

"You know it does."

Something crossed her face, an expression he couldn't interpret, and he braced himself for her to tell him to get lost.

She stepped back from the door, angling her body in an invitation for him to step inside. "I've made marsalos for breakfast. Would you like to join me?"

He went still. Took a breath. It was always a good idea to breathe. "Thank you. Marsalos are my favorite."

It was actually true, marsalos were his favorite, but he knew he'd have eagerly agreed if she'd told him she was grinding up tree bark.

"How did you make them so fast?" He stepped past her, got a sense of color and light from her decor.

"I put them in to bake while I went for my walk," she said as she turned away and walked to the open plan kitchen. "How do you like your jah?"

Her hair was still slightly damp from her shower and it hung in a thick blue curtain down her back, loose and free.

Nick flicked the door shut behind him and followed her.

She picked up a cup, eyebrows raised. Waiting for him to tell her how he liked his jah, he realized.

"Nothing added," he said, and had to clear his throat.

She set the cup under her jah maker and he heard the whirr of the pods being pulverized.

"Fancy machine." He cleared his throat again. "I thought Halatians didn't like jah."

She took a deep sip from her cup, eyed him over the top. "I do. But then, I've lived in Parn since I was ten, which is more than half my life, so you could say I'm more Parnian than Halatian now."

Funny how no one ever seemed to think about it that way. Halatians were Halatians first, in most peoples' minds. "Well, I'm glad you do. I haven't found my jah machine yet."

He forced his gaze away from her long, slim back as she turned to take the marsalos from the oven and studied the pictures on the walls and the furniture.

Her apartment was minimalist, very soothing. On the left hand wall there was a picture, an actual framed picture rather than a screen frame flicking through images, of Nortri.

It wasn't the usual one of him Nick had seen before, the one that always made the Halatian martyr look brooding and a little sulky. This one was a picture taken with Nortri looking straight into the lens and smiling with a sad, but genuine, smile of affection.

"I've never seen this one," he said, walking over to look at it more carefully.

"It's unique," she said, and when he turned, she was holding two plates of marsalos in her hand. "Would you take the jah? I thought we could eat on the balcony."

He scooped up the cups and followed her again, setting them down on the low table between two deep armchairs on her balcony and snagging the first marsalos before he even sat down.

"You really do like marsalos," Tila said.

He chewed, taking it slow because it was still close enough to hot for caution. The sweetness of the tamir chunks and the fruity, juicy bursts of the berries were better than he remembered his grandmother's being.

"I think you just ruined all other marsalos for me. For life." He picked up his cup and sipped his jah.

She smiled, and he realized she wasn't taking him seriously.

"I never joke about marsalos," he assured her. He swallowed down the rest of it with pure enjoyment.

"The house mother in the home I was sent to after I was rescued from the *Caliope* was a baker." Tila's lips quirked. "She considered baking a form of therapy and thought I needed a lot of it. And I wanted to learn how to bake marsalos because . . . well, I wanted to, and she was happy to teach me."

"Do you miss Halatia?" He'd always assumed Halatians did, but now he wondered if she even remembered her home planet.

She lifted her shoulders. "I have vague memories. I was happy. Safe. My mother was killed when the earthquakes started. My father and I managed to get off planet in one of the medium-sized pleasure cruisers with my aunt and cousin, but he died defending us from the smugglers when they took over the ship."

"I'm sorry."

She glanced over at him. "You couldn't have been more than twelve or thirteen at the time."

"I'm still sorry." He held her gaze, and she eventually looked away.

He wanted to ask her if she resented the rest of the Verdant String.

Resented the criminal slowness of their response that had allowed the pirates and smugglers a chance to pounce, to hold the survivors for ransom to the other seven planets while the governments bickered about giving in to extortion and about how many Halatians each planet would take.

They'd focused on everything but the most important issue. The lives of the people in the smuggler ships.

"What do you do?" he asked instead.

"I work for the company that manages the City Run. I'm a systems engineer."

"Do you work in the Hub?"

She nodded.

"I go that way every day, too. It's surprising we haven't shared an EM in that direction yet."

He was watching her face as he spoke, and he thought he saw a guilty expression cross her face.

"You've been avoiding me?"

She closed her eyes for a moment, opened them with a sigh. "I might wait until I hear you leave before leaving myself. Fortunately for me, you start early."

He grinned. "You're really not a fan of . . . tension, are you? And you never answered my question before. Why does it bother you?"

She fiddled with her cup, turning it around and around in her hand. "You could say I'm a little skittish as a result of my experiences. I've had my share of relationships." She looked up, her dark blue gaze like a punch of color. "But when I saw you that first day, outside and then later, in the lift and on the balcony, I was . . ." She looked away, shrugged.

"Overcome?" Nick asked. "Blindsided?"

His words forced a laugh out of her. "Are you usually like this?"

He leaned forward. "I only asked that because that's how I felt, myself."

She'd curled her feet under her, snuggling deep into the comfortable cushions of the chair, mug held in both hands, and she froze in place at his words.

"Did you?"

"Yes."

She relaxed back into the chair. "Well, that's good to know." She sent him a smile that got broader. "Very good."

"Since you invited me in to breakfast, I'm guessing your own reaction wasn't too different."

She hid her smile behind her cup. "Maybe."

He smiled back.

No maybe about it.

CHAPTER 6

"ARE THOSE MARSALOS?" Cris leaned forward and gave the paper bag Nick was carrying an appreciative sniff.

"Yes." Nick extended the bag toward her in silent offer.

"Mmm." She took one, widened her eyes in surprise as she bit in. "Wow. Where'd you get them?"

Nick didn't know why he didn't want to answer. He shrugged.

Always sharp, Cris took another bite, her gaze now focused on him. "You don't know where you got the best marsalos in the city? Marsalos Man himself?"

"A friend gave them to me." He folded the bag--Cris was only getting one if she was going to interrogate him--and sat down at his desk. He set his screen in its holder and checked his messages.

"Where'd she get them?" Cris sat next to him and swung her chair in his direction.

Nick glanced at her, irritated. "She made them."

Chris gave a happy sigh, and Nick noticed her smug grin.

Shit. He'd fallen straight into her trap. Now she knew the friend was a woman and she'd seen him early enough today to give him freshly baked marsalos.

He set his mouth in a thin, tight line and worked through the schedule of open cases he wanted to get through, flicking his screen to projection mode on his curved desk.

"Does she have a name?" Cris was still staring at him, making no effort to even look busy.

He grunted, then made a rude gesture with his hand.

"What?" Vreg ambled over. He had some kind of built-in radar. He always knew when something was going on.

"Nick has a girlfriend who baked him fresh marsalos this morning." Cris leaned back in her chair, and ate the last bite of marsalos. "She's an awesome cook, too."

"Wow. She must really be sweet on you. Marsalos? From scratch?"

Nick closed his eyes, tipped back his head. "Don't either of you have something better to do?"

"As of this second, everyone has something better to do." Commander Drake stepped out of his office into the main working space, his eyes hard. "Suit up."

"Another one?" Nick asked, his gut clenching when Drake nodded.

"An office building on the other side of the city. Explosion on the fourth floor."

They ran through to suit up, each stopping in front of their personal armor and arsenal cubicle, and Drake stalked in behind them.

He was probably timing them.

Nick slammed his laz into its holster, grabbed his helmet and saw Cris was doing the same.

They ran to their hover.

"I'm with you," Drake said from behind him as Cris keyed their usual four seater to open the doors in advance.

Nick turned to look at his commander over his shoulder, hoping his dismay didn't show on his face. "You want to sit in front, sir?"

Drake's response was merely a raised brow and then he slid into a front seat, and Cris, already on the other side, swung into the front next to him, shooting Nick a smug grin.

She programmed the route and the hover shot out of the launch tube. The moment they were out, Nick could see the smoke rising in the distance.

Below them, the track was busy, the EM vehicles stacked one behind the other as people realized the danger and programmed a change in direction away from the Hub.

As Cris took them high and fast toward the explosion, Nick resigned himself to another hellish day.

"Any link between this new building and the others?" Cris asked Drake.

Drake shook his head. "There are fifteen businesses in this new building. There were more than ten businesses in each of the other two buildings hit, some of them with a few hundred employees each, so the connection could be there, we just haven't stumbled across it."

"Casualties?" Nick asked.

Drake shook his head. "Don't know yet."

Cris circled the building, and Nick saw the fourth floor on the north side had taken the brunt of the damage. The building was a living garden, with plants growing up the sides in a riot of fruit and flowers, and the mark the explosion had left looked disturbingly like a physical wound on a living organism. As if it had been pierced in the side.

People were running out of the ground floor doors on all sides, and Nick was pleased to see there were City Watch officers at each exit, directing the survivors to an enclosed space where they could be questioned.

In every other incident, all those people had turned out to be genuine employees in the building, and none had explosives residue on them. But they never knew when they might get lucky.

A perimeter had been cleared around the building, and Cris landed in the pedestrian area in front of the door, empty of everyone except officials.

The three other Protection Unit hovers, each carrying two team members, landed beside them.

Drake was out before Cris had shut the engine down, striding over to one of the officials, his head bent in close as they spoke.

Nick got out slowly, taking in the debris scattered around them. He walked over with Cris to join the rest of the team, and after a minute, Drake called them to him.

"The officer in charge says the flow of people out the building has stopped. Everyone who can get out is out."

That was their signal. Everyone checked their equipment.

Drake handed out instructions, and they broke into groups of two.

Nick got Vreg, and they went through the front doors, moving slowly through the massive foyer of the building. Vreg took the slim, silver search tool out of his pocket and tapped it, and the schematics of the building were projected in 3D in front of them. There was no one on the lower floors, although later someone would come through and check anyway, but there were definitely heat signatures on the fourth floor, the epicenter of the explosion, and a few stragglers higher up, perhaps afraid to come down.

Nick studied the information and then coordinated with the rest of the team, and he and Vreg took the stairwell on the north side.

As they moved toward the entrance to the fourth floor, a smell hung in the air--the bitter tang of the explosive.

He exchanged a look with Vreg before he pushed open the door, but they knew what they'd most likely find.

The teams checked in from their positions at the entry points on the same floor, and they began searching.

A soft exclamation from Cris over his earpiece told him she and Bagins had found the first body.

It took him and Vreg less than thirty seconds to find the second.

Three hours later, they stood beside their hovers, grim-faced and angry.

"Only three unharmed on the fourth floor," Cris said, and she looked back up at the building. "Thirty injured."

"And seven dead, more than in the other two explosions combined." Bagins rubbed a hand against his temple.

"The question is, was it just bad luck this time, or are they escalating?" Drake appeared beside them, as grim-faced as they were.

Nick shrugged. "It was the same charge as before, same composition of chemicals, same amount of explosive. We may discover more from the survivors. If they were having a meeting it might account for the higher death toll."

Drake nodded, looked over at the small crowd of journalists who'd gathered to hear whatever news they could get, and although his expression didn't change, Nick had the sense he was steeling himself for what was to come.

"Get back to the office." Drake looked them over. "And start searching for the connection on how these assholes are targeting the buildings. Don't stop until you have an answer."

Tila didn't take the stairs. She was too tired.

She'd stayed late to finish the project she was working on, so close to the end she hadn't been able to leave, but when she realized the lateness of the hour, and the fact that she'd been staring at her screen for ten minutes without reading a word of the report, she forced herself to pack up and go home.

At least she'd been so late she'd missed the EM logjam caused by the bombing of the Dalcart Building.

Speaking of which . . .

She pulled up short as she turned into her hallway, her gaze on the broad, slumped shoulders of Nick Bartega.

He seemed to be staring at his door.

She moved carefully to her own door, looking sideways at Nick as she ran her finger through the lock.

He stirred, lifting the strap of the big bag dangling from his hand onto his shoulder and turning to catch her eye. "Sorry, long day. I was just thinking something through."

His voice was rough.

"Long day for me, too, but I bet yours was worse. I heard about the Dalcart Building." She was tired, but making dinner for two was no more difficult than making it for one. "Have you eaten?"

He shook his head, and she gestured him into her apartment, walking in and letting him close the door behind them.

She set down her things, and moved to the kitchen, getting out the ingredients she planned to use.

The fact that he wasn't talking struck her after a while, and she turned to look at him.

He was standing close to the counter, bag gone, and she guessed he'd set it down inside his apartment before coming back into hers. He seemed to be completely closed in.

"Problem?" she asked.

He shook his head and sat at counter, watching her.

He looked exhausted.

His hair was slightly damp so he must have showered and changed at work, washing the evidence of his painful day off him. He smelled good, but she couldn't shake the feeling that however solid he looked, he was not himself.

She let him sit quietly as she put the food together. When she slid a plate in front of him, he looked up, blinking.

"Sorry, I--"

She shook her head, handing him his cutlery. "No apology necessary." She took the seat next to him and they ate in silence. The tension she usually felt when he was around had gone, replaced by a quiet restfulness.

When they were done, she took the plates and put them in the washer, and when she turned, it was to find him lying on her long, deep couch, eyes closed.

She hesitated, unsure whether to shake him awake and force him off to his own apartment, or whether to leave him be.

But he was an officer of Commander Drake's Protection Unit, and leaving him to sleep peacefully was the least she could do, beside the more personal connection they'd forged since she'd made him breakfast this morning.

She took off his boots, covered him with a warm throw, and worked a pillow under his head before she made her way upstairs to shower and climb into bed.

There was no storm blowing outside, but as she closed her eyes and snuggled deeper under the covers, she realized she didn't need one to feel safe tonight.

CHAPTER 7

THE KNOCKING WAS MUFFLED but very persistent.

Nick lifted his head in irritation, and then blinked as he registered his whereabouts.

It came back to him, the exhaustion of clearing the Dalcart Building, dealing with the bodies, and then spending the rest of the day until his eyes were burning in his head looking for connections between anyone in any of the three buildings that had been hit.

He'd been standing in front of his door, getting up the enthusiasm to walk through into his mess of an apartment, when Tila had simply taken him in, fed him, and . . . he lifted himself up and grabbed the blanket lying over him before it fell to the ground . . . tucked him in, by the looks of things.

He smiled a slow, sly smile.

Well, how about that?

Whoever was knocking seemed to give the door they were knocking on a kick, and it jerked him back to the reason he'd woken up in the first place.

The knocking wasn't coming from Tila's door, so it must be--

He jumped up and opened the door just as Cris spun around,

screen in hand.

She glared at him. "It's fine. I've located him. I'll call you back now." She lowered her hand. "We've been trying to get hold of you since 4am."

He frowned, and then remembered he'd set his bag inside his door last night before he'd joined Tila for dinner.

"What the hell are you doing next door, and where is your communicator?" Cris's eyes were narrowed in fury.

"Nick, are you okay?"

Nick turned, saw Tila peering out into the hallway, barefoot but in a smart, slim, cream dress, her dark blue hair swinging forward as she caught sight of Cris.

He cleared his throat. "This is my colleague, Cris. I left my communicator in my apartment last night, and they got worried when they couldn't get hold of me."

She smiled then, a sweet, open smile that seemed to catch Cris completely by surprise. "I'm Tila. Would you like to come in for some jah? I'm about to make some."

"I need a quick shower," Nick said to Cris, aware there had to be a reason she'd been dispatched to fetch him from home, but knowing she wouldn't say anything in front of a stranger. "You might as well."

Cris nodded, her gaze darting between him and Tila in a way that had alarm bells ringing in his head, and he edged past her, opened his door, and nearly tripped over his bag as he stepped into his apartment. He took out his communicator and saw there had been ten attempts to contact him since four this morning.

Definitely something going on.

He showered and dressed as fast as he could, made it back down to Tila's, and knocked lightly.

Cris answered.

"That was quick." She stepped back to let him in. "Tila is making us breakfast."

He frowned at her.

"We've got time." She smiled at him serenely. "Now we know

you're safe and sound."

"Why wouldn't I be?"

She shook her head in a quick move that had him burning with curiosity and then she walked back to the kitchen to continue setting places at the small table in the kitchen.

Tila turned with a pile of pancakes on a plate, and gestured him to the table.

"I made you some jah." She sat down beside Cris and he joined them, feeling strange with Cris here, like the smallest mistake could lose him his chance.

"Thank you." He wanted to thank her for last night, too, but that was private, and none of Cris's business.

Tila looked up at him and smiled, that same sweet smile she'd given Cris earlier, and he felt a pang of disappointment. He wanted something more from her. Something . . . else.

"So where do you work, Tila?" Cris cut into her pancakes with a murmur of approval.

"I work in the Hub, in a building designed by Guan. Similar to this one, actually." She smiled as she said it, her affection for the dead architect clear. "It's called Freya's Puzzle."

"Another Puzzle building, huh?" Cris waved her hand. "How did that happen?"

"I worked at Freya's Puzzle before I came to live here. I'd been in my old place for the minimum two years and wanted a change, so I put my name down for Garma's Puzzle. I had to wait a year, but I eventually got it."

"And what about that picture?" Cris gestured to the image of Nortri with her fork. "Were you friends?"

Tila shook her head. "We were cousins. He was older than I was, and when we were rescued, we were all that was left of our family."

There was silence for a moment, because there was nothing more to say about the destruction of Halatia and certainly nothing more to say about Nortri. He'd been the symbol of the plight of the Halatians, his emaciated body and injuries telling the story of the cruelty of the smugglers, and equally, the lack of charity and compassion of the seven remaining planets of the Verdant String.

They'd watched Halatia implode and they had been too slow to act, and that delay had nearly wiped out an entire people.

They were all saved from the moment by a chirp from both Cris and Nick's communicators.

Nick gulped down the last swallow of jah, stuffed the last bite of pancake into his mouth and stood.

"We've got to go."

"Be careful," Tila said, standing herself. "Both of you."

Cris leaned over and kissed her cheek. "Thanks for breakfast, Tila, I look forward to hanging out with you soon." She moved to the door, and Nick leaned forward himself.

His lips brushed her cheek. "Well, it seems Cris is good for something, after all." He spoke almost against her ear, still leaning close in.

Tila laughed. "What's that?"

"Forging the way," he murmured, and then kissed the other cheek, too.

"Goodbye, Nick." Tila drew back, but her eyes danced with humor.

"See you later." He walked out the apartment, and found Cris waiting for him, eyebrows raised, in the hallway. He pointed a finger at her.

"Not a word."

She rolled her eyes. "Like that's going to happen. But moving on to more urgent matters, Drake was attacked last night. It looks like he was specifically targeted, which is why we were trying to make sure every member of the team was okay."

"Is the commander all right?"

Cris nodded. "He's fine. We didn't know about you, though. You gave us quite a turn."

Nick glanced at her. "You going to blab about where I was?"

Cris gave him an evil smile. "What do you think?"

Shit.

CHAPTER 8

TILA STOOD UP AND STRETCHED.

All around her, her team bent their heads over their screens, faces set in concentration.

She felt closed in and edgy. The air wasn't stale, exactly, but it seemed to press in on her.

"Anyone need anything from me for the next hour or so?" she asked. No one looked up, and there was only a single grunt of acknowledgment that she'd even spoken.

Good.

She grabbed her screen, stopped at the machine near the door to make herself a cup of jah, and then walked down the corridor.

She stood for a moment where the passageway kinked strangely, pretending to check something on her screen, and when she was certain there was no one around, she turned the protruding carving of a flower fixed to the wall to the right, and pushed. The wall swung inward, and she stepped onto a deep balcony, with its lush plants and careful screening.

She loved it.

Loved the little present Guan had created for anyone able to solve Freya's Puzzle.

It had taken her six months, but she had managed it in the end. Garma's Puzzle had taken less time, because she knew the way Guan thought by the time she'd managed to get an apartment in his other Puzzle, but this little haven was still her favorite.

She hadn't known the reason for the buildings' names, had only slowly over time noticed the references to Halatian myth and history in the carvings and murals, and had come to realize there was a trail to follow.

She'd kept it quiet when she'd first realized, a secret she'd hugged to herself with a sense of fun and excitement.

She had been such a serious child.

The trauma of her abduction by the smugglers, the death of her parents, the abuse she'd suffered as she'd circled Parn in the smugglers' ship, had led to her barely saying a word for years. Nortri's death had come just as she was emerging from her shell, and it sent her back there for a long time afterward.

But that hadn't been who she was on Halatia. It was hard to remember, but she had the sense she'd laughed more than she'd done anything else. She'd played with her friends. Cuddled with her mother and father.

She hadn't always been the kind of person Nick Bartega had to coax out of her shell.

She pulled one of the deep, comfortable armchairs into the sun, and then settled in, cup in hand, earpieces in place to listen to her favorite music. All set to get lost in her work.

All three of them were dressed as clients, their clothes smart, bags containing their screens slung over their shoulders.

It wasn't a natural fit for any of them, and if they hadn't have been here for three weeks already, and gotten used to the style of clothes and the way people carried themselves, Dun didn't think they'd have pulled it off.

Even so, he felt uncomfortable enough, and exposed enough, to have to concentrate on projecting calm.

This wasn't how they did things.

They worked at night, setting the explosives in advance, but that hadn't been possible last night. The building's increased security had made their planned infiltration impossible.

They were victims of their own success.

Their previous attacks on other buildings in the Hub had led to more vigilance everywhere.

In the case of this one, Freya's Puzzle, that had meant they couldn't get in under cover of darkness.

That hadn't gone down well with the boss.

He'd ordered a quick, unplanned hit on the head of the Protection Unit in angry reaction, but like anything not well researched, it had failed. They had been lucky to get away alive.

Jirmain would try to get to Drake again, though. Dun had seen that look of fanatical hatred on his boss's face before. And the same went for the attack on Freya's Puzzle.

Jirmain would not hear of putting it off, or choosing another target, even though getting in was pushing the edge of safety for his team.

Dun had tried to explain it was a much higher risk to go in so boldly, that if they chose somewhere else, they could come back for Freya's Puzzle another day, but Jirmain wouldn't even hear Dun out.

So now here he was, standing in front of the lifts, with a deadly cargo in his screen bag.

They'd had to assemble the bomb and carry it in already made, which had sweat popping up along Dun's hairline, and he wasn't afraid to admit it.

It was much safer to bring in the pieces separately, assemble it on site, but he couldn't do that in a place as open plan as the firm he had been told to target, in broad daylight, with all the employees present.

He drew in a deep, angry breath.

He was going to ask for double salary for this one. And maybe Jirmain would give it to him.

He knew well enough he had no recourse if Jirmain refused. And you didn't walk away from the organization, either, if you didn't like the terms. He'd seen the bodies of the few who thought they could. And as for the disaster on Cepi . . . he'd been on board the ship that had taken out the team that had failed Jirmain there.

They had been obliterated.

A chime sounded, dumping him back to reality, and the door of the circular lift spun left, opening up. He, Kirt, and Timbo stepped inside.

It felt like a trap, but no client would take the stairs.

"I hate these things." Kirt's grip on his bag was white-knuckled as the lift whisked them upward.

They were all too used to ship life. Being in Var was both exhilarating and strangely nerve-wracking. Planet life was an adjustment for all of them, growing up, as they had, on the smuggler ships.

This was an easier life by far.

The famous citizenship dividend--whispered about in awed, hushed tones by some in the smuggler community, derided by others--was a revelation up close. Everyone had housing, even transportation was free and easy to find.

The downside, the reason two Breakaway planets had come into existence in the last fifteen years, was that no citizen of the Verdant String could horde wealth. Some earned more than others, due to the hours and complexity of their job, but the massive inequalities of the past had been over on the Verdant String for more than fifty years.

The philosophy had started when the first two planets of the Verdant String had sent out space ships and encountered each other. By the time they'd found all eight planets colonized by the same people, it was more than a philosophy, it was a political movement.

If they had all arrived in the five solar systems that formed the Verdant String together from some mysterious other world, and were all responsible for the development of their current successes, then they all had to benefit from its riches.

A tiny percent of the population could no longer hold on to the majority of the wealth.

The Breakaways were called the greed planets, and Dun couldn't disagree. Everyone there was looking for the big break, a pathway to massive power and wealth. Few, very few, attained it, and they did so more through viciousness and violence than any inherent genius or hard work. In the weeks he'd spent in Var, he couldn't swear the Verdant String way wasn't better. Much better.

Not an opinion he'd be voicing to Jirmain or anyone else.

The lift stopped and Dun stepped out into the soothing reception area of the business Jirmain wanted destroyed.

Two security officers were waiting for them.

"Apologies, but due to heightened security concerns, we're checking everyone for explosives," one of them said, a wand in her hand.

Kirt looked over at him, panic on his face, and Timbo pulled his laz.

The lift door closed behind them, shutting them off from a quick escape, and with a sense of doom, Dun pulled his own laz and started firing.

CHAPTER 9

THE SOUND of hovers slowly broke through Tila's concentration. There was a ban on hover use except by officials, and a cold chill ran down her arms.

Had there been another explosion?

She hadn't heard one, so what where the hovers doing so close by?

She set her screen aside, stood, and walked to the balustrade to look out.

The noise was coming from above her, and she looked up, stumbling back at the sight of a hover directly overhead. She stared with wide eyes as it lowered, then stopped when it was level with her.

She looked straight into the eyes of the pilot.

Nick.

She knew her mouth dropped open, but she couldn't help it.

And to say he looked less than thrilled to see her was an understatement.

She tried to smile and gave a little wave, and he scowled at her, lifted the hover up and back, then dived down toward the ground.

She leaned over the edge and saw him land in what should have been a busy street.

It was cleared of all EMs and people, and the chill that had gripped her earlier intensified.

Could there have been an explosion in the building? But she would surely have heard it?

Her screen chimed, and she raced back to it, and snatched it up.

"Nick?"

"Tila, where are you?" His voice was clipped, his face expressionless. She'd never seen him this way, and she suddenly found him intimidating.

The feeling triggered anger, more than anything else.

"What do you mean, where am I? We just looked each other in the eye." She glared back at him, and then walked over to the balustrade and looked down at his hover, to see if she could see him.

He stood beside the vehicle, with three other Protection Unit members around him. They were far below her and she couldn't tell much about them.

Nick took a deep breath. "Where are you in the building? Our plans aren't showing a balcony at your location."

"Oh." She bit her lip. But she'd always known the puzzle would have to come out sometime. "When Guan built his puzzle buildings, he built a series of clues into the murals and decorations, which all lead to a secret room. In the case of Freya's Puzzle, it's this balcony."

There was silence, and she saw Nick look over at one of his colleagues out of the frame.

"How many people know about the balcony?" He turned back to the screen, eyes intense.

"Just me, as far as I know." She shrugged. "I've kept it my little secret."

"What's the access point?" Cris leaned into the frame, her features far more relaxed and friendly than Nick's.

"Hi, Cris." Tila smiled. "The entrance to the balcony is in the corridor just past the main open office, where the passageway kinks."

"Thanks." Cris winked and disappeared from view.

"Tila Dor Rio." The voice that spoke was deep, a little rougher than she remembered, but still unmistakable. Commander Drake must have taken the screen from Nick, because suddenly he was the only one in the frame.

"Commander," she acknowledged, heart beating with a nervousness she couldn't explain. "Hello."

He looked suddenly discomforted. "Hello. I'm sorry we meet again under such circumstances. Would it be possible for us to rappel a team onto your balcony and you to get them into the passageway without being seen?"

"Yes, but I don't understand why. What's going on?"

"You're not hiding there?" Drake frowned.

"Hiding from what?"

There was silence for a moment.

"Three men have taken your colleagues hostage, and they're insisting they'll detonate the explosive they brought in with them, killing themselves as well as everyone in your firm, unless we give them a way to escape."

Tila looked at the time, realized she'd been on the balcony for at least two hours, and yes, it was incredibly strange that no one had tried to contact her in that time. She had no messages from her colleagues at all.

"Is anyone hurt?" Could she really have sat here in the sun and not been aware of any of this?

The Commander paused, and her stomach sank.

"We think a few people are injured, and the two security guards who confronted the men may be dead."

Tila fisted her hands. "Just tell me what you need me to do."

———

Drake was watching him, a strange look on his face, and Nick fought the urge to stare back in challenge.

He would not be made to feel embarrassed for what had just happened. When Tila had moved to the edge of the balcony and looked up, they had thought they were about to speak to a hostage-taker. To find himself staring into Tila's eyes had shocked him to the core.

"So, how do you know Tila Dor Ria?"

"She's my neighbor." Nick could see Drake hadn't expected that answer.

"Haven't you just moved?" Drake asked after a pause.

Nick nodded. "Just over a week ago."

"You seem pretty friendly for having known her a week."

Nick frowned at him and said nothing. What did it matter to Drake how well he did or didn't know Tila?

Drake stared, waiting for a response, and when Nick didn't oblige, he turned and made a 'come' gesture with his hands. The other members of the team crowded around.

"We have a way in, but the civilian does not, I repeat does not, accompany you. She shows you the door to the corridor, and you leave her safe on that balcony."

"Agreed." Drake would get no argument from Nick on that.

"Bartega, you able to think straight if I send you up there?"

It was Nick's turn to narrow his eyes. He gave a tight nod, and tried to ignore the stares of his team mates.

"Wait," Vreg said suddenly. "Is this the marsalos girl?"

Out of the corner of his eye, Nick saw Cris shaking her head at Vreg, trying to cut him off.

"Marsalos?" Drake swung around, surprise and shock on his face. "What's this about, Bartega?"

Nick cleared his throat. "Tila makes really good marsalos, sir."

Drake studied him for a beat, and Nick glimpsed something in his eyes--some deep-felt emotion--before the commander turned back to the group and started laying out the plan of action.

They were up in the hover fifteen minutes later, Drake piloting, and one by one, they slid down on ropes to Tila's secret balcony.

She stood back against the wall as they came down, giving them as much space as she could in the delicate, beautiful space.

The intricate tile work that was a feature of Guan's style was on full display, and the architect had built planters into the design and filled them with lush flowers and miniature trees.

Nick was the last to rappel in, and he found Cris introducing the team to Tila. They were all a little too curious, a little too focused on her, in his opinion.

"What's the plan?" Tila didn't greet him, and after the tension of their earlier conversation, he supposed he didn't blame her. She focused on him, eyes unwavering, but he could see the tremble of her hands.

Cris was standing beside her and she slid an arm around her shoulders. "We're going to try and get your colleagues out safely, Tila. Trust us."

Tila looked up at her and nodded, face serious and lips in a tight line.

Nick cleared his throat. "If you show us how to get into the corridor, we'll do the rest. You stay back here." Nick waited for her gaze to land on him again. "Don't come out until the commander or one of us calls your comm and lets you know it's safe."

She gave a reluctant nod. "Well, getting you to the corridor is easy enough." She gestured toward the wall, which seemed to be nothing but a wall to Nick, although it was covered in plaster flowers, trees, birds, and insects in a relief pattern, white against a wall of deep blue.

Tila reached out, grabbed a flower, and twisted it, and the thin outline of a door emerged.

She leaned against it, opening it a fraction, and then gave a nod, stepping aside so Nick could get through.

He stopped as he passed her, wanting to say something, but his entire team was looking on.

She stared at his chest, and then the stiffness left her spine. "Stay safe," she murmured, just as she had done this morning, but this time, it was she who leaned toward him and brushed a kiss on his cheek.

His gaze snapped to hers, and then Cris was crowding him, moving him on, and he stepped out into a section of passageway that kinked strangely. He slid along the wall, the rest of the team right behind him, silent and focused.

Up ahead, there was a scream, and Nick stopped moving, listening carefully.

The scream was followed by a shout, and he began edging along the wall again, getting closer to the noise.

"What have you done to her? Where. Is. Tila?"

Nick tensed. They'd all hoped that the rest of the staff had not brought the hostage-takers' attention to the fact that Tila hadn't been rounded up, but possibly they thought she was injured, rather than hiding.

This could work for them.

If some of the hostage-takers came looking for Tila, they could pick them off, one by one.

He heard the murmur of voices, and then he winced as a voice boomed over what must the in-house speaker system in the office.

"Tila?" The man speaking dragged out her name, almost singing it. "Apparently you're out there somewhere on this floor. I have someone here called Yasmi, and I'm going to have my colleague hurt her until you come out. If you don't come out at all, I'll discharge my laz against her throat. I'm assuming your hiding place is tricky, or we'd have found you already, so I'm giving you until the count of fifty. Starting . . . now."

Nick turned to the team, face grim as the man started counting down. Over the sound of his voice, all of them heard the short, sharp cry of someone being struck.

They were dealing with pros. They'd known this from the start, but these insurgents were obviously smart enough not to split up and weaken their position.

Movement at the back of the team had him raising his gaze, and there was Tila, standing in the open doorway to her secret space, face pale under the warm gold of her skin tone, hands shaking.

"I have to go," she said, voice raw. She was looking only at him.

"No--"

"I'm going, Nick." Her voice trembled, then steadied. "You can take advantage of that by putting some cameras on me somewhere, so you can get some visuals of the hostage-takers and the setup in the conference room, or not. But I'm not letting him kill Yasmi. I don't think he's bluffing."

Unfortunately, Nick didn't, either. If Tila didn't come out, they would kill Yasmi, and then start on the next person in the room. They had enough hostages to spare.

He and Vreg shared a look, and then Nick gave a nod. Vreg started to move instantly, pulling two tiny, pinhead sized cameras out of his pack.

Cris took them from him, fixing one to the back of Tila's cream dress high on the right shoulder, so they could see what was happening behind her, and one just below the dress's V neck at front.

All the while, the countdown droned on over the grunts and cries of someone being beaten up. Tila looked as if she was taking the beating herself.

Nick touched his comm. The commander looked out at him from the screen. Drake would have heard and seen everything from the cameras in their uniforms and packs.

"I don't like it." There was a palpable tension on Drake's face.

Nick nodded. "Me, either."

Cris cut in. "She's ready."

The counting was down to twenty-five. Halfway.

Nick could see Tila was visibly agitated. She wanted to get moving. Stop her friend's torture.

"Having eyes on the room is a good thing," Cris reminded them. "We're not going to be able to pick them off, not if they're this risk averse, so having a good idea where everyone is before we storm in is the best way to go. Especially if they're hunkering down and not splitting up."

She was right, but handing the hostage-takers a new hostage was not procedure. And procedure or not, Nick did not want her going in there. Every part of him screamed that it was a bad, bad idea.

Drake's face reflected his own thoughts.

"Sir?" he asked.

"Let me speak to her."

Tila stepped toward him, face set. He put out a hand and touched her arm. "The commander wants to speak to you."

She looked down at the screen. "Sorry, Commander. I have to go."

"I know."

Nick couldn't see Drake, Tila was holding the screen, but the commander's voice was deep and steady.

"Just stay calm. Keep your wits about you. The team will get you out."

She nodded, handed the screen back, and Nick covered her hand with his.

"Your turn to stay safe," he murmured in her ear, and she took a deep breath, gave a nod, and then ran down the passageway.

CHAPTER 10

"STOP! I'M HERE." Tila raced past the open seating of the office to the sounds of Yasmi in pain, and rounded the corner to the reception area and the conference room.

The two bodies lying near the lift made her stumble to a stop.

She stared at the two security officers in horror, and then movement to her left made her turn. She saw her own shock mirrored in those of the two men at the conference room door.

She blinked.

Why were *they* horrified?

The sound of Yasmi receiving another blow forced her toward them. "Stop! I'm here."

The door to the conference room was open, and the two men, each armed with a laz, stood in the doorway, one outside and to the right, the other inside and to the left.

The one inside turned and made a movement with his hand, and the sound of fists on flesh ceased.

They watched her approach, neither making any move to grab her or touch her in any way.

She'd been expecting some violence, some jostling, but they

moved aside, gazes tracking her every move in silence, and let her walk into the room on her own.

She felt the weight of their gaze, and flashed back to her youth, when she often felt eyes on her wherever she went.

It had taken a long time to shake the constant sense of being stared at.

It affected her choice of exercise clothing--everything she wore, in fact--although in the case of work, instead of wearing baggy clothes to hide in, she made sure she knew what was appropriate so as not to stand out.

It was as if these men remembered the Halatian Incident like it was yesterday, and the weight of their emotion sat as heavily on her as it did on them.

She glanced back at them, and then away when she saw they were still staring, forcing herself to concentrate on her colleagues instead.

Everyone was there, three lying against the back wall, obviously injured, with a few other colleagues crouched beside them. The rest of were sitting on the floor, all crowded together, faces turned her way.

Yasmi was sitting on one of the conference room chairs, her lip bleeding, both eyes already swollen, her dark skin mottled and bruised.

"I should have kept my mouth shut," Yasmi said, slurring her words a little as she tried to talk around her split lip, and Tila saw her teeth were coated in blood. "I thought you were lying injured some-where and needed help."

"This isn't your fault, Yasmi," Tila said. She looked over at the man who'd been hitting her tall, curvaceous boss, her eyes narrow.

The man was staring at her the same way the other two had, and Tila forced herself to ignore him. She walked to Yasmi and offered her hand to help her up.

After a moment's hesitation, Yasmi took it, and then Tila helped her to the back of the room to sit with the other injured.

Tila did a slow turn as Yasmi sank down, hoping the cameras were picking up every angle for Nick and his team.

The three hostage-takers were standing together now, talking in low voices. Their gazes were still on her. The one who'd done the countdown, the obvious leader of the group, seemed to be dressing the other two down.

Perhaps for not finding her? She was afraid to stare at them too long and attract even more attention, so she turned to her friends and colleagues, huddled together, and sat among them.

"Where were you hiding?" Ahn whispered, eyes avid with curiosity.

She shook her head, not answering. The team may well have retreated back there to study the footage she was supplying and make their plans.

Rescue was coming. She knew that for a fact, and she would be ready when it came.

Dun flicked his gaze between the Halatian woman and his comm screen. His hand trembled a little.

He couldn't contact Jirmain. The Protection Unit would have decryption tech, and he couldn't risk them tracking where the comm was going, or what was said.

So he would have to make the decisions himself, put himself in Jirmain's head and pick a plan.

The problem was, Jirmain was not . . . he was going to say sane, but that wasn't it. Jirmain was sane enough, but he was unpredictable. He could find something funny one day that would send him into a rage the next.

You never knew which way he was going to jump.

Dun had come to understand he did it on purpose, and he couldn't really fault the logic. Jirmain was at the top of the pile because of it.

Dun also knew full well that if he didn't get himself and the team out soon, Jirmain would find a way to make sure they never got out at all.

The clock was ticking.

He was almost surprised the building hadn't collapsed around them already.

Just a few months ago, Jirmain had destroyed an entire complex of ancient ruins on the tiny moon of Cepi, along with a priceless piece of tech, just to shield any trail to himself, and he hadn't cared how many people died while he did it.

That had been the turning point for Dun.

He'd watched the ruins collapse, standing on the control deck of their slick new ship, and known that he had better never be in Jirmain's way, because his boss would think nothing of riding right through him.

He also knew if he left the Halatian woman here and Jirmain found out about it, he might as well tip back his throat and hand Jirmain his laz, because he would not be forgiven.

"Do you think the boss knew?" Kirt asked softly. "About her?" His head jerked toward Tila.

Dun shook his head. "He wouldn't have chosen this target if he'd known. Or he'd have had us grab her first."

"What do we do?" Timbo shuffled nervously.

"We use the plan we were going to use on Cepi," Dun said, feeling his way through the idea.

"That didn't work out so well." Kirt cleared his throat.

"No, but the circumstances were a little different. We have a Halatian, and no one is going to want her hurt. Taking one hostage is simpler, and such a high-value one is perfect."

"So, we walk out with her?" Timbo frowned. "How?"

"I'm thinking," Dun said. And he knew he better think fast. Jirmain would be coming for him, just as much as the Protection Unit of Var.

CHAPTER 11

"EVERYBODY UP."

Dun, the leader of the group, stood over Tila, his fingers drumming against his thigh. There was something about the movement that spoke of nerves, and she pulled herself warily to a crouch.

All around her, her colleagues stumbled to their feet.

"Yasmi, too?" she asked Dun, her arm going behind Yasmi's shoulder to help her up.

"No." Dun stepped back. "The wounded stay where they are. Everyone else, come to the middle of the room."

While he spoke, one of the other hostage-takers, Kirt, picked up a bulky screen bag and laid it carefully on the conference table.

He opened the bag and took out a slim, silver box, then looked over at Dun.

"Set it for ten minutes." Dun walked to the window, looked down. "No, make it fifteen."

Kirt seemed to relax a little at that.

And then Tila understood.

They were setting the timer on the explosive.

Her horrified gaze went to Yasmi, and the three others lying beside her.

"We could carry them," she said as Dun turned away from the window.

His gaze focused on her, and he looked her over for a long, tense beat. "No. They'll give the Protection Unit something to do. If they're as good as they say they are, the PU will have them out before it goes off."

"Are you arming the bomb?" Ahn's voice rose as he stared at the device on the table.

His words created an immediate reaction, gasps and cries of fear.

"Quiet!" Dun lifted his laz. "Or I'll make sure a few more of you are injured and have to stay here."

There was dead silence.

"Come here," he said to Tila.

She hesitated, and he shifted his arm to point his laz at Carin, the tiny, bubbly office administrator.

Tila came.

He grabbed the back of her dress, pulling her back against his chest, and she felt the cool metal bar of the laz against her spine.

"Start the countdown." Dun's voice was a little less steady as he said that.

They're afraid, Tila realized. They aren't invincible.

And Nick and his team could hopefully see and hear everything that was happening in here. She twisted a little in Kirt's direction as she thought that, so the camera would record what he was doing. He touched the device and then turned, face tense, and nodded.

Dun gave a signal, and Kirt and the third member of the team, Timbo, came to stand with her and Dun. They stood so that Tila was in the middle, with the hostage-takers forming a circle around her.

"Everyone, gather around us."

Her colleagues didn't move.

Dun lifted his arm again and fired at Rei, the stocky information systems analyst who worked a few desks from her. He went down with a cry, holding his leg.

Everyone went utterly still with shock.

"Move! Every second you delay is a second your injured friends won't have to get out before the explosive detonates."

The words galvanized everyone. They shuffled forward, and soon they were a tight crowd, with Tila and the three hostage-takers in the center.

"Hook arms with someone to your left and your right." Dun waved his laz to attract everyone's attention. "Try to run, and we'll shoot. You've just seen how I'm perfectly happy to do it. Maybe we'll hit you, maybe we'll hit one of your friends instead. At this distance, we'll probably hit more than one." His voice was calmer now, and he kept his tone soft, so everyone had to be quiet to hear him. "Does everyone understand me?"

There were a few nods.

"Good. Move to the door."

They shuffled forward, and Tila looked back at Yasmi and the others, propped against the wall, at Rei lying pale and panting on the floor.

Their faces were pinched with fear, and the anger that had been burning in her licked higher.

Someone at the front opened the door and they spilled out into the reception area, and came to a dead stop.

Tila tried to crane her neck to see what was going on, but her view was blocked.

"Protection Unit," Nick called out. "Put down your weapons and surrender."

Relief sang through her just at the sound of his voice, but Dun was directly in front of her, and Tila saw the thick muscles in Dun's back tense and his fists bunch.

He would not go down without a fight.

"I would suggest *you* put down *your* weapons." Dun's words were cool. He lifted his laz, moving it almost lazily as he swung around and shot Ahn, standing close to her, in the leg.

He cried out and Tila reached for him, trying to grab him as he fell.

There was panic in the group now, they were on the verge of running, fear driving them more than Dun's threats.

He must have realized it. "You and you," he pointed at two young info techs. "Take him into the conference room."

His words were calm, the order matter-of-fact, and the tension notched down a little. He jerked his head at Timbo, and then made a sign with his hand, and the big hostage-taker followed the two techs as they got their arms under Ahn's shoulders and half-carried him into the room.

"No need for anyone to get hurt," Nick's voice was rock solid and soothing. "We'll retreat."

"Good." As Dun spoke, they all heard two more shots, and the cries of Ahn's teammates.

"We're moving back." Nick's shout came from further away this time, and Dun's attention was focused toward the passageway but he turned his head when Timbo stepped back out, closed the door behind him, and gave Dun a nod.

"Don't let it be said I'm not generous." Dun raised his voice to a shout so Nick could hear. "You have," Dun looked down at the time, "eleven minutes until the explosive detonates and eight injured to evacuate. One for each member of your team. Now stay back until we're gone, or we'll injure a few more, and then you'll have to choose who to save."

"Agreed," Nick called after a moment's silence.

What choice did he have?

"Get in the lift," Dun ordered, and they moved toward it immediately, no hesitation now. Whoever was leading took a slightly angled route. It confused Tila until she remembered the bodies of the security officers on the floor.

She breathed through the nausea that suddenly gripped her.

When the lift doors pivoted open, they stepped in, jostling each other, but there were too many of them to fit.

Five of her colleagues were pushed out, and then the lift doors spun closed. Her friend Sarta was forced up against her, and Tila gripped her hand in solidarity.

They were swept downward to an empty lobby.

"Out."

The group, much smaller now, lurched like a demented spider to the building's entrance, and then they were in a street as empty as the lobby.

"Go right." Dun clamped his hand on Tila's shoulder, his grip tight, as if he expected her to run.

They moved in their strange shuffle and lurch beside the EM tracks, and Tila caught a glimpse of a barrier up ahead.

People were pushing against it, craning to see what was going on.

"Don't slow down," Dun's hand on her shoulder tightened even more, and he touched his laz to Sarta's throat. "Head straight at the barrier. They'll let us through."

"What if they don't?" Timbo asked.

Dun raised his laz. "They will."

The injured hostages were all out, and the dull black containment box around the explosive shook and then emitted a thick, foul-smelling smoke.

"Threat contained." Cris spoke into her comm unit and then turned to cough.

Nick didn't feel as if the threat had been contained at all.

Dun and his crew were on the streets, and they still had ten hostages.

He signaled to Cris that he was going down, and then took the lift, his gaze on his screen, watching Dun force Tila and her colleagues straight at the barrier with a sense of dread and powerlessness.

Tila's camera was blocked by Dun's back most of the time, but he caught glimpses of the City Watch officers. They held their posts, their expressions tense, while the crowds behind them tried to work out what was going on.

The lift reached the ground floor, and Nick ran, glancing down at his screen every few steps.

Just before the hostages reached the barrier, one of the officers put his hand on his laz, and Nick had the perfect view of Dun reaching for his own weapon, lifting his arm up from the middle of the hostage group, and shooting straight into the onlookers behind the barrier.

The flash of the laz, the screams of the people as two victims went down, created a panicked reaction, and the crowd began shoving as they tried to flee.

The hostages hit the barrier, and then they were through it, amongst the wild crowd.

The impact of their arrival was like a stone dropping into a pond, displacing people in a ripple around them, but then the group broke up, and Nick sped up as he saw from the camera footage that Tila was still sandwiched between Dun and Timbo, but they were moving much faster, shoving and pushing their way through the crowd.

He caught a glimpse of another of Tila's colleagues, Sarta, with a laz to her throat, and guessed they were using her to secure Tila's cooperation.

But why?

Nick had seen the hostage-takers' reaction when Tila had stepped into the foyer. They'd been shocked, and then they'd regrouped. Ever since, they'd behaved as if she was a prize.

"Bartega."

The call came from his left, and Nick looked over to find Drake running just behind him, and catching up.

The commander held a screen as well, and Nick guessed he was viewing the same footage.

"There." He pointed up ahead. "They're taking her down a side street."

Drake's face was hard to read, but he was another whose reaction to Tila seemed more intense than Nick could explain.

He fell into step with Nick, breathing a little harder, perhaps, but keeping up.

Tila seemed to have decided the time had come to stop cooperating because they started dragging her along, and then there was a cry, and she twisted her body, the camera catching a glimpse of Sarta being shoved to the ground and left behind.

"They've let the colleague go," he called to Drake. "Tila's the only hostage they have left."

Drake picked up the pace, and Nick matched it. He had to concentrate on his footing now, rather than the screen, as they reached the corner and saw Sarta Falcon pulling herself up to a sitting position on the street, and a number of people coming to her aid.

"Which way did they take her?" Drake barked at her, and she lifted her head in shock, took in the uniform, and then pointed with a shaking arm behind her.

Nick looked down at the screen, but all he could see now was Dun's back and Timbo's front.

Tila stumbled, and a flicker of movement told Nick that Timbo must have reached out an arm to steady her.

There was the clatter of feet on stairs, and the camera jiggled as Tila was herded downward, and then there was darkness.

"I can't see," Tila whispered.

And then she went quiet.

The screen went black.

Nick looked over at Drake. "We've lost her."

CHAPTER 12

TILA'S EYES struggled to acclimatize to the darkness, and she closed her eyes.

She felt hands on either side of her head, and then something was jammed down, like a tight crown.

She cried out, more in surprise than in pain--although it had hurt--but no sound came out of her mouth. She snapped open her eyes, but rather than being able to see better, it was as if she were in a black pit.

A snuff.

She bet they'd shoved a snuff on her head.

The wire headgear was used on prisoners, to keep them blind and silent during prisoner transfers, although they were used more in popular fiction than in real life, she was sure.

Her head would be surrounded by a forcefield that allowed nothing in or out.

She shuddered in a breath.

Someone ran a hand over her shoulder, making her flinch away, but whatever they had to say was lost on her.

After a pause, one of them took her by the upper arm and began to lead her forward.

She balked at moving without seeing where she was going, lurching stiffly as she was propelled forward.

She sensed someone leaning in closer, as if to speak to her, but if so, they'd forgotten she was in her own little null zone.

She drew in another breath, trying to keep herself calm as she stumbled over her own feet. She thought there was a vibration under her feet, as if she was in a lift.

She couldn't see, but hopefully Nick could. As long as the snuff didn't affect the cameras, they'd be able to see where she was.

To come for her.

It was the only thing she had to hold on to.

The Halatian woman's panic, her fear, hesitating with every step she took, worried Dun.

This was one of those situations where he didn't think he could win. She wouldn't come with them voluntarily, so she had to be treated as a prisoner, as a hostage, but at the same time, Jirmain would not want her hurt in any way.

There was no good way to abduct someone, but Jirmain wouldn't be reasonable about it.

The only reason Dun continued on was that he knew Jirmain would be even less reasonable if he didn't bring her at all.

He got tired of watching her timid movements and scooped her up, feeling her shock as she was suddenly swung into his arms. He strode toward the hover on the roof, his arms tightening as she struggled.

He placed her as carefully as he could into the back seat and she leaned away from him, hands clenched at her sides.

"She's trouble." Timbo was staring at her, his face stone cold.

"Agreed." Dun rubbed a hand over the pocket that contained his laz. "I wish I'd left her wherever she was hiding in that building."

Kirt made a sound. "Could we just . . . leave her?"

Dun shared a look with him, then Timbo. Saw that maybe if he'd put it to them when they were back in Freya's Puzzle, maybe they could have worked out a deal of mutual silence, but now . . .

He shook his head. "There'll be coverage. The boss would have seen her in our group when we made a break for it through the barrier. The information stations will have filmed it."

Kirt closed his eyes and pinched his nose. "I'd forgotten that." He shuddered, as if thinking through what would have happened if they'd tried to pretend she hadn't existed.

"So we have to take her." Timbo's voice was flat.

"We have to take her. We have to be careful with her." Dun lifted his shoulders in a shrug. It was what it was.

He looked out from the rooftop. There were no hovers in sight, the action all happening behind the massive buildings that were a barrier between this one and Freya's Puzzle.

"Looks like we'll have a clear run," Kirt said, following his gaze.

Dun nodded. At least one thing was going right. "Let's go."

There was something wrong with Tila.

She hadn't said a word, made a sound, since she'd been forced into a dark basement, and Nick noticed a jerkiness to her movements that was unlike her usual fluid grace.

The tiny cameras on the front and back of her dress were still working though. The hostage-takers had moved through the gloomy space as if they knew where they were going, and then they had herded Tila into a lift.

The lift opened into some kind of atrium, and Tila's camera showed her moving slowly to a door and then out onto an open roof. Nick didn't know why he felt such a wash of rage when one of the men picked her up and carried her in quick, purposeful strides to a hover.

"I see it," Drake said.

They were standing at an intersection, trying to work out from the feed which building the insurgents were in.

"Send a hover to our position," Drake was saying into his comm set.

Nick saw the three men standing beside the hover, looking inside at Tila, and his heart beat a little faster.

What were they discussing?

The look on their faces was hard to read.

The big one looked like he'd just as soon throw her off the roof than take her along, the other two looked more worried than enraged.

They seemed to come to an agreement, and then they climbed in.

They were taking her with them. As backup in case they were pursued?

Nick's head snapped back, looking upward.

He heard something, a faint whine, and he ran to the corner and looked up. Saw the glint of sunlight on the wing of a hover as it tilted to the right.

He looked at his screen quickly, saw the camera at the back of Tila's dress was recording a limited view of the buildings they were flying over, as if she had wedged her back up against the window.

She was trying to give them something to go on.

He caught a glimpse of the arena, and felt the thrill of the chase.

The insurgents had had things their way for the last three weeks, but now, they were the prey, and Nick was coming for them.

CHAPTER 13

THE SNUFF LIFTED off her head, and it took Tila a long time to regain her senses. For a few panic-filled moments, she was afraid they wouldn't come back at all.

Eventually she heard the low voices of the three men, and her eyes slowly adjusted to the muted light of a single fixture on the side of a large building.

Somewhere close by, she heard a shuttle take off, and she turned in its direction.

"You're back." Dun sounded relieved, his gaze fixed on her, and she hunched her shoulders.

"We're away from the city, clearly." She turned around, hoping the camera would pick something up, but the only building she could see was the big one next to her. The darkness was deep around them, but she could smell trees, and hear them, she realized as her hearing improved. She could hear the sigh of the wind in the trees. "Why not just let me go?"

Dun shook his head. "That's not up to me."

"Where are we, then? Where are you taking me?" She hadn't been able to speak until now, but if she could get them to give her a location, that might help Nick--if he was close enough to be in range for the transmitter.

She didn't know how strong the signal was, but it had to have a limit, and if Nick wasn't close enough . . .

She shook off the thought, waiting for Dun's reply.

"Our boy's on duty," Timbo said, suddenly looming behind Dun.

Dun twisted his head around, gave a nod. "Let's go."

He put a hand on her upper arm, curling his fingers around it, the grip strong, and pulled her along with him.

She resisted, surprising him, and she thought he was going to yank her, but he didn't.

"I can put the snuff back on," he said quietly. "It'll make things more difficult for me, but my job is to work around difficult things, so I'll deal. What I will definitely do if you don't cooperate, keep your mouth shut, and pretend to be a voluntary part of this group is that wherever I end up, or how it ends, I will make sure Freya's Puzzle gets another explosive, and I'll be sure to specify that it goes off in the middle of your office."

There was silence between them for a long beat.

"Am I being clear?" he said at last.

"Yes," she whispered.

"Good." He sighed, as if she'd somehow forced him to threaten her friends and colleagues against his will, and then started walking again.

She kept up, rounding the corner with him into a brighter light and the landscaped front of what seemed to be a massive warehouse.

Another shuttle took off close by, and this time Tila could see the purple flare from the engine and the flash of lights along the wings as it rose into the night sky.

They walked inside, and Tila realized the building contained hovers and shuttles behind a massive transparent wall, and a smaller section with offices and counters.

They headed for one of the counters and Dun's grip on her arm tightened.

The man standing behind it looked their way, and his focus sharpened on her.

"Hello, Fry," Dun called as they approached.

"Picked up a guest?" Fry asked Dun, but his eyes stayed on her.

"Just a favor for a friend," Dun said easily. "I hope it won't be a problem?"

"No." Fry shook his head. "We can just adjust the log."

"Actually," Dun leaned against the counter on his elbow. "I'd like to let the log stay as is."

Fry frowned. "Regulations state you can't fly in any shuttle, even if you aren't planning to go spaceward, without sampling in. In case of a crash. We need to know who's in every shuttle."

"I know, but I want you to make an exception for me." Dun smiled at him, and slid a hand into his pocket. "Like you did for us before."

Fry was still frowning. "I can't make an exception."

"You're obviously a principled man," Dun said and pulled out a thin rectangular crystal. He pushed it across the counter with a finger.

Fry's gaze flew to Tila, eyes wide, as if she could somehow explain what was happening. She looked back at him with a blank expression, too afraid to do anything else.

She hadn't ever been in a shuttle, but she knew that you had to offer up a small blood sample before you boarded. Dun was right to worry. As soon as her bio-sig appeared in the system, Nick would know where to find her.

If he hadn't already worked out where she was from the camera feed.

"What is this?" Fry looked down at the crystal.

Dun looked momentarily disconcerted. "It's a crystal chip. Like the one I gave you before."

"Oh." Fry bent closer.

"There's a lot of money on those chips, Fry, incentive for you to keep the log as it is."

"No one can get into that shuttle without a sample." Fry lifted his hands up. "We could be closed down if we allow it."

He looked over Dun's shoulder, surprise in his eyes and the frown back on his face, and then he collapsed.

Tila gasped and looked behind her, saw Timbo putting away his laz.

"That was going nowhere," he said to Dun.

Dun sighed. "Agreed. I keep forgetting people on this planet aren't desperate enough to take a bribe. Tuck him up against the counter so it's hard to see him." He started walking toward the shuttles, his grip on her arm even tighter. "I really wish you hadn't been at work today," he said to her.

Tila stared at him coldly. "Believe me, the feeling is mutual."

They had the airfield location.

Nick flicked the coordinates onto the hover's screen, and it banked right.

It was already set to its fastest speed.

"Why are they taking her?" he asked Drake, who was sitting beside him. "They're must believe they're free and clear now."

The commander had spent a lot of time on his comm set, dealing with the aftermath of the Freya's Puzzle hostage situation, but now he was quiet, looking at the images from Tila's camera feed as she was dragged into a large warehouse and taken to a small shuttle.

"You're right." Drake looked up. "And they've said a few things, expressed some regret that they even came into contact with her. It's like they're taking her almost in spite of their feelings on the matter."

"That big one, Timbo, would just as soon put a laz to her throat and finish her. The other two would rather leave her behind." Nick watched as Tila was shoved into a seat on the shuttle. "It's as if they resent her."

Drake said nothing, his gaze fixed on the screen as the footage coming from Tila's camera jerked, and tilted upward. She was in the air now. Flying away at incredible speeds.

They wouldn't be able to catch them, so they would have to find out where they were going to.

Cris's voice broke through on the hover's comm. "The medics found the shuttle company employee who was shot. He's alive. One of his colleagues will meet you at the airfield."

Ten minutes later, Nick saw the big building up ahead. It seemed better lit now than it had been when Tila was here.

They landed the hover in front of the entrance and Nick took a moment to check the security arrangements. They were almost non-existent. This was a shuttle port that dealt mainly with in-planet rather than spaceward flight.

It was a clever move by Dun.

The security was never that heavy for in-planet travel and they'd become even more complacent since the end of the Faldine War.

The war had been over for two years, and had never spilled over into Parn, but everyone had been on alert while it raged, knowing any planet in the Verdant String could be targeted.

Nick looked down at his screen, saw it was blank.

It was inevitable.

The transmitter on the camera was only so strong.

They'd lost her.

He looked over at Drake, saw he was scowling down at his own screen.

"Protection Unit?" A woman called from the entrance, hands fluttering nervously. "I'm Mev."

Her words snapped Nick's attention back to the problem at hand. He strode toward her, and Drake fell into step with him.

Inside, two medics crouched beside a man lying on a stretcher. He was unconscious.

"What do you know about what happened here?" Drake asked Mev, his voice a whip crack.

"I . . . I don't know much." She looked at her colleague on the ground, and then back at Nick, eyes brimming with tears. "Fry told me there were some men who were strange. They made some strange joke that didn't feel like a joke and gave him a weird crystal thing."

Nick frowned. "What was the joke?"

"They asked him to alter their entry point. They came in from off-planet, and we have to submit the coordinates of their entry with Shuttle Management to make sure it's safe." Mev lifted her shoulders in confusion. "You can't change it. It's already sent to SM before the shuttle even comes through, in case there's another shuttle too close which poses a danger of collision."

"So these men didn't understand how the system worked?" Drake asked.

She nodded.

"Where is the crystal they gave him?" Nick asked her.

"Fry gave it to our boss. Or rather, left it in his office. The boss is away for a few days, so Fry is . . . was in charge."

She showed them to the office, and Drake gently picked up the slim crystal chip.

"A credit chip?" Nick had never seen one. That was more Corruption and Fraud's area, but he'd heard of them. "They're mostly used on the Breakaways, aren't they? Or when we trade with non-Verdant String planets?"

Drake nodded. "Trade and Foreign Interaction use them, but they're strictly regulated." His eyes were grim. "The crime lords on the Breakaways use them, and the smugglers."

"They thought Fry would take a bribe, and that he could somehow change their entry coordinates." Nick looked down at the crystal. "They aren't Verdant String."

Drake nodded. "If they're from a Breakaway, they're incredibly ill-informed on how Verdant String works. The only people who could possibly be that out of the loop are people who moved as children to the Breakaways when they were established ten years ago. It's that, or they're smugglers."

Nick stepped out of the office, caught Mev's eye. "Can you give us the coordinates they wanted Fry to alter?"

She nodded. Walked to a screen behind the counter, and Nick tipped his screen closer so she could flick the information over.

He looked down at the numbers with the first flare of hope.

They had somewhere to start looking. Somewhere the insurgents had been trying to hide.

CHAPTER 14

TILA LOST count of the hours she sat in the shuttle.

At some point she dozed off, fear and stress draining her of energy.

The thought that looped around and around in her head was that taking her didn't make any sense. They could have left her in the warehouse beside the shuttle, no one there had tried to stop them leaving.

There had to be another reason. Something to do with the way they'd stared at her in Freya's Puzzle.

Something to do with her being Halatian.

The thought ramped up her distress, because she didn't have to stretch her imagination very far to guess they were smugglers.

A new generation of them, around about her own age.

And she could imagine to some twisted mind, the decimation of the smuggler gangs after the Halatian Incident could be laid at the feet of the Halatians themselves.

They were distinctive enough, rare enough, to make a good scapegoat.

And while the smugglers may have reestablished a small foothold in the fifteen years since they'd chosen to make money out of massive tragedy and human suffering, their survival was only thanks to the establishment of the Breakaways.

They had been hounded after Halatia imploded, chased down in every corner of the Verdant String and beyond.

There had been nowhere for them to hide until the two planets that became the Breakaways were discovered ten years ago and claimed by two huge corporations willing to cut ties with the Verdant String for the promise of massive profit.

That hadn't worked out too well for them, but it had given the smugglers a place to hide. A lawless, unpatrolled area to hunker down, regroup, and use as a base.

She had a horrible feeling Dun was taking her to whatever dark corner of the Breakaways he called home.

They weren't out of Parn's sovereign space yet, though.

The Mother and Child were clear from the window beside her seat, the Mother blocking all but a slither of the Child from view, as if protecting it.

They were heading straight for the Mother, and she started paying more attention as they got closer and closer.

There was a strange sense of having been here before, as if time had wound back fifteen years.

The *Caliope*, the smuggler ship she'd been imprisoned on, had lurked here while the smugglers demanded ransom for the Halatians onboard, hiding in the deep chasms on the Mother.

If she'd had any doubt about who Dun, Timbo and Kirt were, it was put to rest now.

They dropped down toward the surface of the Mother as if they were planning to slam the shuttle into her barren wastes, but the closer they got, the more clear the topography became. Hills, mountains, valleys and deep gorges.

The shuttle dove down into a wide chasm fashioned from dull gray rock and then slowed, lowering down to land on the uneven floor of the canyon.

Dun cursed as the ship wobbled and then leaned a little to the side.

"What did you expect?" Kirt asked him. "That they would have bothered to set up a landing pad?"

Dun snorted out a cynical laugh.

Timbo said nothing, but Tila thought he looked like he shared the joke.

She had the sense whoever 'they' were wouldn't be that much of a joke to her.

They waited, and she wondered what for until she heard the whine of an engine. The sound of a clamp engaging echoed through the shuttle, and then Dun moved forward, waited for the lock-light to blink on, and hit the button to open the door.

All Tila could see was a circular tunnel.

Rather than put on suits and go outside under their own steam, they were being fetched in some kind of vehicle, she realized.

"Come on," Dun said.

Kirt went down the tunnel first, and Dun waited for her to get up from her seat and step into the tube.

He was so close behind her she could feel his breath on her neck.

She flinched, and tried to move a little faster.

The tunnel was short, and she stepped into the back of what looked like an all-terrain vehicle with two rows of seats facing each other. Kirt was already sitting down.

Two people stood on either side of the doors, a man and a woman, and they reacted with surprise at the sight of her.

Dun walked through, gave them a nod, and when Timbo stepped in, the two newcomers tore their gaze from her and began unclipping the all-terrain from the shuttle.

"Sit," Dun told her, and she moved to a seat in the middle of the row and did as she was told.

For now.

There were no windows at the back of the all-terrain, so Tila didn't know where exactly they'd brought her, but she assumed they had reached their destination when the driver swung around and reversed, and the two crew members reconnected the tunnel.

The trip had been teeth-rattling, but short. Too short.

She wanted more time before she faced whatever it was she had to face.

Something unpleasant awaited her.

She knew it. Everyone in the vehicle knew it.

The tension was palpable.

If her *kidnappers* were afraid for her, she honestly didn't know what to expect.

When she forced herself to stand, her legs felt unsteady, and she had to deliberately straighten her spine and push back her shoulders.

She put a hand out to steady herself as she walked down the thin, echoing metal cylinder and all but stumbled into a massive cargo space.

Dun was right behind her again, and his hand shot out to steady her, his hold solicitous rather than cruel.

A few of the waiting crowd gasped at the sight of her, and someone pushed through from the back, taller than most, and with the same striking hair color as her own.

"Dun." His voice was neutral, but Tila could see Dun swallow nervously.

"Jirmain." He inclined his head.

"Well?" Jirmain stared at her, eyes narrowed, and she watched him back.

She had to admit, seeing a Halatian had lifted her spirits for a moment, but then she'd noticed the way the others had reacted to him.

They were genuinely afraid of him.

Being Halatian herself, she didn't carry the baggage the rest of the Verdant String did about her fellow Halatians. They weren't just victims or delicate flowers in need of protection. They could be just as wonderful, and just as awful, as anyone else.

"Tila Del Rio worked at Freya's Puzzle." Dun said nothing more.

Jirmain flicked his gaze over to Dun for a moment, then back to her. "How long have you worked there?" he asked her.

"Four years." She would have liked to have told him it was none of his business, but it wasn't important information. She'd save her *fuck-you's* for when they really counted.

"Who did the recon for that building?" Jirmain asked. There was silence. And Jirmain pointed to one of the people in the crowd. "Who, Hart?"

Hart looked a little wild-eyed. "You, Jirmain."

Jirmain lifted a screen from his pocket and flicked through, frowning. He must have found something he didn't like, because he seemed to stare daggers at the screen. When he looked up, there was something almost feral in his gaze. "Bring her, Dun. We'll talk somewhere more private."

Dun clamped down on her upper arm again and moved her forward. The crowd parted, gazes avid as she walked between them.

They were a rag tag bunch. The slick clothes Dun and his two colleagues wore stood out in contrast to the majority of the onlookers, whose clothes were old, ragged and patched.

Dun marched her out of the loading area and into a long passageway. The metal was dark and dull, although clean enough, and their footsteps rang and echoed as they walked.

"A bit different to what you're used to, eh?" Dun said, looking over at her with a sly expression.

"No, I've been in a place like this before," she answered. "My father and my aunt died in a place just like this, and when I was rescued, I weighed almost half what I should have weighed for my age. My cousin, the only family I had left, killed himself because the memories of his time in a place like this were too terrible to bear."

His face went blank and he didn't talk again.

She didn't know if she should have provoked him like that or not.

But she couldn't regret it. With every step she took deeper into the ship, more memories of her captivity assailed her.

Her breath was short, and her legs trembled by the time Dun touched a panel beside a door and then ushered her in when it slid open.

Jirmain stood beside a table, looking down at his screen.

"You did well to get her out, Dun. Is that why there was no explosion?"

"Yes." Dun didn't seem to go in for long explanations. Tila wondered if it was his natural manner, or whether it was an attempt at self-preservation.

"I rushed you."

"You did." Dun didn't color his tone as he said it, walking a strictly neutral line.

At his agreement, Jirmain turned, eyebrow raised. Then gave a smile. "Occasionally someone does need to tell me I'm wrong. I forget that, sometimes. You must be tired after everything that's happened. I'll deal with Tila Del Rio from here."

Dun nodded and walked out, abandoning her without a word.

She didn't have any reason to feel betrayed, but she did. She saw him turn just before the door swished closed behind him for one last look before leaving her with Jirmain.

So he felt it, too. That he was leaving her to her fate. And he felt a little bit bad about it.

She turned back to face Jirmain, and they stared at each other in silence.

"Which smuggler ship brought you to Parn?" he asked.

"The *Caliope*."

He drew in a quick breath at that. "I don't remember you."

"I was in a cell with some other girls my age most of the time."

He gave a slow nod. "How old were you? Nine?"

"Ten," she said. "You must have been about fourteen?"

He gave a nod.

"So how did you end up here, and not on Parn?" Tila hadn't

known there were children who were never saved. It was almost inconceivable to her.

"The few smugglers who escaped took some of us as hostages."

"But when they were out of danger, why didn't they sell you back?"

He lifted a shoulder. "It was too risky for them. The tide had turned so hard against them, there was no civilized place they could go to negotiate our release that would have been safe for them. They decided it was easier to just keep us."

"How could that be? Surely you were missed?"

He shook his head. "It wasn't as if they had a passenger list." His smile was wry, almost friendly. "No one knew we were missing, because no one knew we were there in the first place."

"But they're not keeping you now," Tila pointed out. "You seem to be in charge."

"Yes." He smiled again, and she saw a flash of something a little crazy, a little unbalanced, in his eyes. "That's the thing about child slaves, they grow up."

"Are there others like you?" Tila asked.

"No." He looked out of a window that showed nothing but black. "There were only two other Halatians, and they didn't survive."

His voice was dismissive. He either didn't care, or cared too much.

"What has this got to do with you killing people on Parn? And why did Dun bring me here?"

Jirmain leaned back against the wall and crossed his arms over his chest, a smug smile on his face. "I'm dishing out some revenge. Fifteen years ago, while we lived and died in misery floating above Parn, the Parnian government argued and disagreed on what to do about us. They could have done the right thing, but it took pictures of our circumstances to convince them to act, and even then, Captain Drake had to go against orders to launch the first offensive."

She looked at him with dislike, and he lifted his shoulders in answer.

"All right, so I'm not telling you anything you don't know from very personal experience." His tone turned bitter. "Not that you suffered the full consequences, like I did." He took a deep breath, and she wondered if he heard the accusatory note in his own words. As if he blamed her for being saved. The thought chilled her.

She was here, right in front of him, and the faceless councillors who'd dithered and prevaricated at the risk of her life and his were not.

If he was looking for an immediate target, she was a little too handy.

She looked up when he went silent, and found him watching her strangely. "My point is, who has paid the price for what they did?" He looked her up and down. "Certainly not the people who left us to die, that's for sure."

"I still don't understand—"

"I'm targeting the business investments of the people who sat on that council. The men and women who served their five years and then went on their way, untouched by the tragedy they helped to create."

Tila lowered herself into a chair. Her legs just couldn't hold her up any longer. "You may be putting a temporary halt to their businesses, but Parn is part of the Verdant String." She looked at him in astonishment. He surely couldn't be so ignorant. "There will be no lasting economic consequences to them. There is no lavish lifestyle you'll be taking away. Economic equality is the watchword of the Verdant String. There's a limit to the amount of money any one person can amass. It was like that on Halatia before it was destroyed. You must know this. The only thing you've done is kill and maim innocent people."

He stared at her for too long, his face blank. "I understand the concept of economic equality. I'm reducing the businesses they've touched to rubble to draw attention to them. I'm taking away their reputations. I'm reminding people of what they did."

"A media campaign could have done that."

He snorted. "No. The only way to truly ram it home was for innocents to lose their lives because of decisions *they* made. That is what will be remembered. A media campaign would be forgotten in a week, a month at most. Massive loss of life, as you know only too well, tends to linger in the mind."

She tried to work out if he was serious. Because if he was, he was stark raving mad. "How will people connect the deaths to those business owners' past decisions when no one knows why you've targeted the companies you have?"

He pushed himself away from the wall. "I may have been a little too subtle for the ham-fisted Drake and his cohorts. I was hoping their investigation would reveal the truth, and coming from them, would have a bigger impact than my simply stating it. But that obviously hasn't worked out."

He walked closer, looming over her, and cocked his head to one side. "Maybe I'll get you to enlighten them."

CHAPTER 15

THE COORDINATES WERE USELESS.

The satellite that was dispatched to the point Mev had given them showed no ships at all, and when Drake pulled strings and got Nick and himself on a special forces fighter and a journey to the exact spot, it was to find nothing.

Just the Mother and Child a short distance away, and then the wide open space that was the rest of Parn's sovereignty.

"They could be anywhere," Nick stared out of the window.

"Not anywhere," Drake said. "Unless they've pinched their way out, they're here somewhere. All satellites are looking for that shuttle. And it'll be somewhere on camera. There isn't a single part of our outer atmosphere that isn't covered. It's just a case of finding the right feed."

What he didn't say, didn't need to, was that the shuttle was a common model, and there were perhaps thousands of them exiting the atmosphere every hour. Finding one specific one would take a long time.

Nick still didn't understand why Dun had taken Tila. It didn't make sense, and the possibilities he thought of sat queasy and slick in his gut.

There were no pleasant scenarios.

He thought of her looking at him over a cup of jah, the wicked, laughing expression in her eyes, and idea that the people blowing up the Var Hub had her in their power had him swallowing hard.

He saw Drake's hands were fisted until the knuckles were white as he looked out into space, and the questions he had back in Var came rushing back. "What is your relationship to Tila?"

Drake tipped back his head and gave Nick a look that did not invite further conversation.

But Nick wasn't backing off. There was something going on here and it was important. He'd already seen that when Drake spoke to Tila at Freya's Puzzle.

"I have no relationship with Tila," Drake said at last.

"Bull. Shit." Nick stood, unable to sit still a moment longer. Everything was too much. Tila's life was in danger, and Drake was lying. Lying through his teeth.

"It's true. I haven't seen her in fifteen years."

Again, there was no way . . . "So you have met her before."

Drake looked over at him. "I rescued her, Bartega. Of course I've met her before."

Nick stood, mouth open. "You mean you personally rescued her? This whole time I was thinking in terms of you leading the team, that she was rescued by some faceless Special Forces officer, but you . . ."

"I broke down the cell door where she was held and carried her out." Drake looked away, out the window. "With a few stops along the way." His smile was faint.

"You never saw her again?" Nick couldn't believe it. Not the way the two had interacted with each other.

"That interfering house mother of hers wouldn't let me. Said whenever anything to do with the rescue was mentioned, she'd get visibly agitated." He shrugged. "It's not that I didn't believe them. But Tila sent me comms. She wanted to speak to me."

"Did you reply?"

"I did. I don't know if she ever got the messages."

"Why did you react like you did when Vreg mentioned she made me marsalos?"

Drake actually looked down, and Nick forced himself to sit, to project more calm that he felt.

"There were two shooters, the guards from that part of the hold, I think, and they didn't care that I had a little girl in my arms, they shot anyway."

"At a child?" Nick breathed it out long and slow.

Drake flicked him an irritated look. "Yes. You didn't get that the smugglers didn't care about the lives they held, they just cared about the money?"

Nick frowned.

"We were pinned down, Tila and I. I managed to squeeze us into a gap between a air filtration unit and the wall and we waited there for them to get cocky, to come looking for us. I wanted to leave her in the hiding place, go hunting, but she wouldn't let me go. She just looked at me with those huge blue eyes, that crazy blue hair wild around her face, and I couldn't leave her. And so we had a quiet chat over the roar of the laz fire and even some old-fashioned projectile shooters that must have been a hundred years old or more.

"She didn't flinch once. She'd gone beyond fear and out the other side when it came to the shooting. The only thing she was afraid of was that I'd leave her.

"And in that conversation, she asked me what my favorite thing was, and I told her marsalos."

Drake drew in a deep breath. "She didn't know what marsalos were, so I had to explain them to her."

"And she grew up and learned how to make them," Nick said softly.

"So it seems." It was Drake's turn to stand. He leaned against the window, and then looked down the length of the shuttle, to where most of the members of the special forces team were gathered.

"What was Tila's favorite thing?" Nick asked.

Drake looked over at him and shook his head.

Something told Nick it wasn't that his commander didn't know the answer, it was that he could no longer speak.

"Commander?"

Drake pushed away from the wall, turning toward the speaker with a sudden, sharp focus.

"There's some news in from Var." Lieutenant Intoh leaned in from the pilot's deck. "You'll want to see this."

She lifted her handheld screen and flicked the information to the comm screen fitted to the back of the ship.

The six other special forces officers looked up from their own screens, and they all focused their attention on a journalist pointing to one of the damaged buildings.

"The insurgents have just released their first statement. They say they'll make an announcement in half an hour."

Intoh lowered the sound as the journalist went on to list all the damage caused in the city.

"This is the first we've heard from them in the nearly four weeks since this started. What are the chances that they speak up just when they get their hands on Tila?" Nick tried to keep the worry out of his voice.

No one replied, because it was pretty much a given that Tila had tipped the balance.

"But why?" Stru, one of the special forces team asked. "What is she to them, that they went to such trouble to take her?"

Drake scrubbed a hand over his face as his only answer.

"They didn't plan to take her when they started out." Nick sat down, his fingers steepled together. "They were there to blow up the building, they got caught, and I'm guessing they were trying to work out a way to get away and still blow something up. That was up until they saw Tila. I saw their reactions on the camera feed when she walked toward them. They were astonished. And they were scared."

"Scared of her?" Hine, another of the team asked, surprised.

Nick shook his head. "Not of her, but of something. Her being there had consequences for them, and by their reaction, not good ones. It was almost as if from that point, their strategy changed."

"To what?" Stru asked.

"To taking her with them."

"What could they have seen in one glance that would have caused that reaction?" Intoh asked.

Drake raised his head. "Her blue hair." His lips thinned. "My guess is they're smugglers. And they want her for no reason other than she's Halatian."

Nick agreed with that, he'd been thinking it for a while, he just didn't understand why.

Up on the screen, the journalist had been replaced with an expert on the Halatian Incident, discussing the shock of having a Halatian abducted right from under the noses of the Protection Unit, and the irony of Commander Drake heading that very unit.

Nick winced, and no one made eye contact with Drake.

But the talking head on screen brought up a good point. Why would the smugglers raise their heads and cause this kind of trouble, just when the political will to stamp them out had begun to fade, after years of intense policing. This would stir things up. Remind people what they'd done, all those years ago.

Why would they want to go there again?

"Why am I really here?" Tila looked over at Dun as he handed her a cup of tea and pushed a small plate of food across the table to her.

Jirmain had ordered him to 'make her comfortable', and Dun had taken her to what looked like a small guest room with a shower and spare clothes. He'd given her twenty minutes, then returned with food and drink.

"You're Halatian." He shrugged.

She twisted her still-damp hair into a single, thick rope, and pushed it over her shoulder. "There are plenty of Halatians in Var. Why me?"

"You were the one we had access to. You were right in front of us. And that's not true, by the way. There aren't plenty of Halatians in Var. You were the first one we'd seen, and we were there for three and a half weeks."

Tila shook her head. She was part of the Halatian Interests Association. Almost all Halatians were. So perhaps she had a better sense than most how many Halatians lived in Var, but she often saw Halatians on the street. "Even so, I really don't understand."

"He's got a thing. A manifesto." Dun's lips twisted a little in a wry smile. No need to clarify who 'he' was. "He thinks the Halatians are all being coopted into the rest of the Verdant String. Phased out, he calls it. Mixed with other Verdant String populations, and diluted into no longer existing as a separate group."

Tila gaped at him. "You took me to be his future partner? So we can have pure bred little Halatians together?"

Dun shrugged. "He hasn't outright stated that, but he did tell us all Halatians we came across were to be brought to him. I don't know if he wants to make little Halatian babies with you, specifically, or whether he just wants to have the option of that. He nearly got some Halatian women a few months ago, on Cepi. Except he had to make a decision that had a high likelihood of killing them to save himself. He chose to save himself." Dun glanced over at her. "So I suppose his manifesto only goes so far."

Tila went cold, not because of the information that Jirmain wasn't as committed to her well-being as he was to his own, that was already a given, but at the mention of Cepi. "That was you? Jirmain and you? On Cepi?" The appetite she'd had for the food in front of her disappeared. Doctor Nyha Bartali and her wards *had* nearly been killed on Cepi four months ago, when the whole moon had been attacked by unknown assailants. They'd barely escaped with their lives when the ruins had been destroyed by a mysterious ship.

"Am I on it now? The ship that blew up the Cepi ruins?" she

asked. She'd seen the footage. The sleek, black ship, mysterious and powerful.

He hesitated, then gave a quick nod.

"But that whole Cepi thing wasn't just to grab Doctor Bartali and her wards, was it?" There were surely far easier ways to get hold of Halatian women.

Dun shook his head. "No. But their presence there was an added bonus. You Halatians are the perfect hostages. No one wants to take any risks with you. But he never intended to let Bartali and her girls go when he got what he wanted."

"Only he didn't get what he wanted, did he?"

Dun's face changed, became harder. "No. And he had to choose. Kill the team on the ground or take the risk that when they were captured, they'd talk. If they'd given up his name and those of his backers, the resources he needed to do what he's doing right now on Parn would have been withdrawn, so he chose to kill."

"Some of those people were your friends?"

Dun flicked her a neutral look. "Some of them. There used to be a certain tradition of loyalty. If you were on a job and it went wrong, every effort would be made to get you back. Jirmain chose the easiest way for himself, in order to stir up trouble on Parn. Since the Break-aways became more established, but especially in the last few years, the patrols, the hard stance against the smugglers, has eased. But he had to have his revenge. Again, for himself alone, and to hell with what's good for the group as a whole."

The bitterness was thick in his voice.

She had to be able to use this. To use the venom.

When she looked up, Dun was watching her, a knowing look in his eyes. "Yes, I don't like what's going on. But don't count on me. You've got a life for yourself in the Verdant String, with your universal citizen's dividend. On this ship, and back on the Break-aways, it's only the vicious who survive. Where I come from, you have to be able to fight your way through anyone who stands in your path, even if they *are* your friend. And you . . . well, you're not my friend."

CHAPTER 16

"DIDN'T you do this with Nyha Bartali on Cepi?" Tila asked Dun as he led her back down the passageway. "Force her to make an announcement?"

He stopped so suddenly, she ran in to the back of him.

"I'd forgotten that." The look he sent her over his shoulder was considering. "But you're right."

They had reached a door, and he turned back to open it, then stepped back so she could precede him.

Something in the expression on his face told her he was . . . not excited, but somehow gleeful about the fact that what was about to happen was similar to what happened on Cepi.

Was it because, like her, others might remember that, and link the two incidents?

That would presumably be bad for Jirmain, something she had come to realize was one of the few things that would make Dun happy.

On that, she was in agreement with him.

"Welcome." Jirmain rose up from a chair, his eyes on her, taking in the clothes Dun had given her. They were clean but worn, a thin shirt and comfortable pants, and a threadbare jacket. He'd also found her comfortable shoes with worn soles.

The chair Jirmain had been sitting in was behind a bank of screens set in a sleek, expensive looking comms station. They must have cost serious money, and some of the equipment was unfamiliar to her. It looked military in origin.

Whoever was giving Jirmain money wasn't being stingy with it.

"Sit."

She walked to the chair he pushed out and sat, turning to face him.

He was still standing, looming over her. "I hope I don't have to threaten you, or tell you not to say anything that would give our position away. This is being recorded, so we'll do it again and again until I'm happy with it. And I don't like having my time wasted." He kept his a smile on his face and his tone pleasant as he spoke.

She wanted to hit him. She looked down in surprise to find her hands in fists.

Huh.

She'd never in her life wanted to commit violence so badly.

It wouldn't do her any good. But outthinking them?

That was something she could definitely try.

"What do you want me to say?" she asked, keeping her tone friendly.

"Tell them the councillors who made the decision to delay rescue during the Halatian Incident are the link between the targets, and tell them the fact my team couldn't blow up the company in Freya's Puzzle means that you will never be returned. You're the consolation prize."

She was watching him as he spoke, and she snorted out a derisive laugh as he said the last sentence. "Right, because that shows how much you believe in Halatian freedom from abduction and imprisonment."

Jirmain frowned at her. Considered her words. "Maybe that is better not spoken aloud," he conceded. "Just leave it at pointing out they are the link. I'm after their reputations, now that it would seem too difficult to return and finish the job."

She nodded, flicking a quick glance at Dun. His face was carefully neutral again, but she could only imagine that Jirmain's casual dismissal of a plan that had put Dun, not Jirmain, in the crosshairs, was just another nail in Jirmain's coffin.

"The public in Var, on the whole of Parn, I imagine, is waiting, Tila." Jirmain gestured to a screen. "Speak."

"My name is Tila Dor Rio. I was abducted from my place of work earlier today by the men responsible for the explosions in Var. They tell me that the reason behind the explosions is revenge. Their leader is a Halatian who was held in the *Caliope* fifteen years ago, and was taken away by smugglers who escaped when Commander Drake and his team infiltrated the ship to rescue the prisoners. He was brought up as a slave, and has worked his way into a position of power among them. He's targeted the men and women who sat on the Parnian Council during the Halatian Incident for their delay in making hard decisions while Halatians died or survived in misery. I was on the *Caliope* myself, although I was lucky enough to be rescued by Commander Drake, and I now find myself in the same place, all over again."

Jirmain shot her a dark look and signaled to someone behind her, presumably to cut the recording.

"What was that last part?" he asked her. There was a tremor in his voice that had the whole room go silent.

"You want to evoke the feelings of the Halatian Incident, don't you?" Dun asked, his voice cutting through the quiet. "Remind everyone how it was, how they felt?" He shrugged. "Her saying that she's back in the same place again is going to do just that."

Jirmain kept looking at her, his eyes curiously blank and dead. After a long moment, he drew in a deep breath through his nose and nodded. "Although you're hardly back on the *Caliope*, are you, Tila?"

She leaned back in her chair, trying to slow her runaway heart without making it obvious. "No. I'm also not ten years old anymore.

And the accommodations may be better, but the confinement still feels the same."

Again, the room was silent, and Jirmain's fists bunched. He wanted to hit her almost as much as she wanted to hit him, she saw with what was almost detached interest.

She was playing with fire, and she was frightened enough to wonder at her own recklessness.

"I don't know where we are, I don't even know what your ship looks like. Let me go, or this excuse of revenge is proven to be so much bullshit."

He didn't like being called out in front of his crew, and he didn't want to admit that he was no longer the downtrodden boy he'd been. He had choices now, and he was making them with open eyes.

"Take the recording and send it," he said to the thin woman who sat at a station a little way from Tila. She'd been giving Tila filthy looks since she'd come in.

She wanted to lean over and tell the woman she didn't want Jirmain, he was all hers, but she didn't know if it was sexual jealousy motivating the dislike, or whether, like Dun, she saw Tila as the embodiment of the pure Halatian Jirmain was trying to avenge, risking the lives and livelihoods of his crew to do it.

"Sure." The woman picked up a screen, spun in her chair and stood up. She walked out the room without a backward glance.

"I'm looking forward to seeing what the reaction will be." Jirmain chuckled, behaving as if the tension in the room had dissipated, when Tila thought it had only increased.

Her and Jirmain's little argument had made it clear to the smugglers in the room what Jirmain had just done.

Put a target on their backs once more.

"Someone is trying to reach you, Commander Drake. One of the victims from Freya's Puzzle. She won't say what it's about." Intoh leaned into the room again, and Nick tore his gaze from the screen and Tila's face, her announcement almost on continual repeat as shocked reaction to her statement reverberated around Parn.

Drake's face was almost gray, and Nick remembered Drake's conversation with Tila when they'd found her on the balcony at Freya's Puzzle and later, Drake's reaction when he heard about Nick's friendship with Tila.

Drake and Tila knew each other, not just because they would have heard each other's names before in connection to the taking of the *Caliope*, but in a deeper way.

Looking at Drake, Nick wondered what Tila was to him, that he would look so sick at the sight of her giving an announcement under duress.

"Commander?" Intoh repeated.

Drake seemed to come back to himself. He stood. "Thanks. I'll take it."

Nick stood with him, walking behind him to the comm station in the pilot's cabin. Intoh gestured to the correct screen.

A woman looked out at them, and Nick recognized her as the person the hostage-takers had thrown to the ground before they'd raced off with Tila. She bit her lip in agitation, and he could see she'd been crying.

"This is Commander Drake."

"Commander, I'm Sarta Danubi. You might remember me as the person lying in the street earlier today. I told you which way they'd taken Tila. I know you're looking for her, and I just wanted to say that I think she was trying to give us a clue to where she is in her message."

Nick's attention was suddenly focused completely on Sarta's face.

"What do you think she's trying to say?" Drake kept his voice calm, but Nick heard the tension in his tone.

"She often stared up at the Mother and Child for minutes at a time, and I asked her just a couple of weeks ago about it. She said that the smugglers flew around Parn during the Halatian Incident, but they also used to hide in the canyons and gorges on the Mother. When she said she's back in the place she was before, I think that's what she meant. She's somewhere on the Mother."

Drake blinked. "Thank you, Sarta. That's helpful. Please don't discuss this with anyone else." His voice seemed to gain strength as he spoke.

Sarta nodded, and Intoh cut her off.

"It's been fifteen years. We took the *Caliope* when they were just outside the upper atmosphere, doing one of their orbits of Parn, and I'd forgotten about the Mother." Drake snapped his fingers, pointed at Intoh. "There were Special Forces maps that we made at the time, plotting where we thought they were going to ground on the Mother. We had strict orders not to engage, so we couldn't get in closer, and we never actually hunted for them on the Mother, but we knew they were bedding down there more often than they were circling Parn. We definitely plotted our best guess as to their movements. I want those maps."

Intoh considered him for a moment. "I'll ask." She didn't move though, standing beside the comm station as if waiting, and Nick finally got it.

"You want us to go."

"If you don't mind. I'll need to speak to my commanding officer."

Drake drew himself up. "I can get those maps through other channels, Lieutenant. Especially now. From the Minister of Defense through to the president, I'm pretty sure I'll have their ear. If Special Forces makes me take the slower route, I will be very vocal in my criticism." He turned on his heel, and walked out.

Intoh watched him go with undisguised shock on her face. She turned to Nick. "I'm sure General Tarr will give him everything, no problem. It's protocol for me to speak to him privately, though. Why would he threaten Special Forces? He's a legend to most of us."

"Maybe he's considered the best because the lives of the people he pledged to protect were more important than Special Forces orders when it came down to it." Nick held her gaze. "He defied his superiors to save the Halatians on the *Caliope* fifteen years ago. Superiors no other captain questioned. It could have gone wrong for him, but instead, he made Parn the face of action and compassion in the Verdant String, when we all know it was just one man's action and passion."

"Don't forget Darline Xan." The pilot up front swiveled her seat toward them.

Nick nodded. "Darline Xan is a hero, but her job was to investigate what was going on, and she managed to find a way to do it despite overwhelming odds. Commander Drake's job was to observe only. He didn't do his job. He did his duty. He cared more for the lives on the *Caliope* than his orders, and we continue to bask in the glory of his heroism. Now one of the people he risked his life and his career to save is in the same position again. Of course he's going to threaten Special Forces if they don't cooperate. He's been down this road before."

"I always wondered why he left Special Forces after the Halatian Incident," Intoh said softly. "I thought it might be because he lost two of his team. I never thought it was disgust at SF itself."

"I'm pretty sure General Tarr knows the real reason," Nick said. "And it's never comfortable knowing someone thinks you're a moral failure. Tarr was also a captain in the SF during the Halatian Incident, wasn't he?"

Intoh gave a tight nod.

"There you go." Nick gave a shrug. "Drake knows Tarr might block him, given the history between them. Personally, I hope not. I hope General Tarr can see a woman's life is on the line, and act accordingly."

Intoh stepped out of his way, so he had a clear path to the door. As he passed her, she murmured, "I hope so, too."

CHAPTER 17

"COMMANDER, WE HAVE THE MAPS." Intoh walked into the rear of the ship and sat down in front of the big screen at the back. She switched off the feed from the news channels on Parn and flicked across a file from her handheld.

Drake stood as the maps flashed onto the screen. "Have any trouble getting these?" he asked.

Intoh said nothing, but from the thin line of her lips, Nick guessed she'd had to use Drake's threat on Tarr and she hadn't liked that he'd forced her to do it. She'd hoped Tarr would behave better, and he'd let her down.

"I'll take that as a yes." Drake sent her a quick, almost apologetic glance. Then he focused on the screen in front of him. "Ah, yes. It's coming back to me. We thought we saw them going in here a few times." He pointed to a deep gorge and then stepped closer, tapping the screen. "They used more than one spot, though. Changed it up. After a while they realized we weren't going to go after them. They got cocky, more or less taunted us, and that's why we were able to get the jump on them in the end. They didn't expect us."

"Ever think that they didn't expect you because you were actually going against orders at the time?" Stru asked.

"Did we think they had someone leaking information to them?" Drake asked. "Yes. Though that wasn't why I did what I did. But it helped that I had no official backing in the end, rather than hindered me. Special Forces tried to spin it that it was all part of the plan afterward, but that fell through pretty quickly."

He sounded like he was talking about an interesting case he'd had nothing to do with, whereas Nick knew he must have known he risked his own and his team's life, and all against orders.

His respect for Drake had always been high, but he had to admit seeing the maps, understanding what the situation had been like, that respect had increased.

He could see the same on the faces of Intoh's team, as well. They were impressed, and every one of them was questioning whether they would have had the nerve to go against orders in such an audacious way and pull something like Drake had done off.

"So where do you think they could be?" Intoh drew them all back to the present with a bump.

"One of four places. My suggestion is we go in very quietly, and send a team to each place. Whoever finds it calls the others, and we try to infiltrate."

Intoh walked up to the screen herself, studied the places Drake had lit up with his pointer.

"All right." She turned to her team. "Two to a team."

"We're coming too," Nick told her. "That's why we're here."

"That goes without saying." Drake crossed his arms over his chest and he and Intoh stared at each other for a long moment, in a silent battle of wills.

"You'll have to get dispensation, Commander. You get killed on this mission, it's my butt in the sling."

"You'll have full immunity, Lieutenant," Drake promised her. "I'll get it now."

He walked into the pilot's cabin, and for a moment there was silence among the team.

"How personal is this?" Stru asked Nick.

Nick looked over at him. "Pretty personal."

Stru frowned. "How does Drake know her so well?"

Nick shifted uncomfortably. He waited a little too long to answer. "He was obviously part of the team who rescued her."

"This isn't personal for Drake, it's personal for you." Intoh had picked up on his mistake, her eyes narrowed, her tone accusatory.

"Tila Dor Rio is my next door neighbor."

They all leaned back, shared quick, neutral looks.

"You two really want to be involved in this?" Stru asked. "It's never a good idea to be in on something when there's a personal element . . ."

"That's so much bullshit and you know it," Nick held his gaze. "You telling me it's not personal for you if one of your team is hurt or captured in the line? That every time you all step out there you aren't on some level worried about your teammates?"

There was silence.

"I thought not. I want Tila safe. No one cares about that more than I do."

"That's where you have it wrong." Drake was back, flicking a file from his screen to Intoh's. "There are your guarantees, Lieutenant. And let's be clear. My priority is getting Tila free. My guess is, your priority is capturing the smugglers who've been blowing up the Hub."

Intoh inclined her head. "That's true. My orders are more skewed to capture than rescue."

"Then let Bartega and I handle the rescue, you can engage the smugglers to your heart's content."

"I can get behind that." Intoh looked down at her screen, nodded when she'd checked the file. "We'll send Stru with you in a team of three. We keep silent until and unless we come across the smugglers."

"Where're we going to land?" Stru asked.

"On the dark side," Intoh told him.

They landed in a hover so silent, Nick and Drake shared an impressed look. Nick was sure Drake was thinking the same thing he was—they had to get one of these for the Protection Unit.

Once they were on the ground, they each got an individual hover of their own, and Nick liked that even more. It didn't so much as hum.

He followed Drake and Stru, letting them take the lead while he hung behind.

The terrain was far rougher that it seemed from the air, the hills were higher, the valleys deeper.

Something in the way the light reflected off the sun, then off the Child, and then onto the Mother, he'd heard. Whatever the reason, it played tricks with the eyes and they decided to keep their height far higher than any of them would have liked. It was better to hug the ground, but better still to be alive at the end of the journey.

Drake had chosen the target they were going to, and from the way he held himself in check, the suppressed air of excitement about him, Nick was sure he'd picked the location he thought most likely to be where the smugglers were hiding.

It was no surprise, then, that after an hour of flying, they settled down their hovers and crept to the edge of a high gorge to find a sleek black ship nestled between the dull gray walls.

"Is that . . .?" Stru breathed out on a gasp.

"The ship from Cepi. It's the ship from Cepi." Nick couldn't take his eyes off it.

Everyone in the Verdant String and beyond had seen the feed from the Kalastoni battleship that had swooped down on Cepi to save an Ankhoran Special Forces team and the Halatian woman Nyha Bartali, only to come face to face with a sleek ship of Verdant String origin but with technical modifications that were unusual to say the least.

It had been fast, too. Destroying the ruins and then pinching away into the black, leaving nothing but questions behind them.

"It's not showing up on any of my instruments." Stru pushed back, away from the edge, and flicked through his tiny screen.

"They've set themselves to maintenance mode, or to dead," Drake said. "There'll be nothing coming in or out, which means they're either all there is, or they're on their own with this mission of theirs. Sink or swim."

"What does that mean for us?" Nick asked.

He saw Drake's smile through the glint of Stru's screen off the glass of his helmet. "Well, given our good luck in finding them, it means they won't be able to see us. They're hoping they're invisible down there. Their ship is black and non-reflective, they're hidden in a deep canyon, and they aren't emitting a single signal."

"Finding them really was incredible luck."

Nick saw Drake's faint smile as he turned back to Stru.

He just stopped himself laughing.

Sure it was. Incredible luck that Drake had gotten to choose which spot he wanted to investigate before the other teams had picked theirs.

"This find is huge." Stru toggled on his comm. "Lieutenant, we found them, and take a look." He lifted up a little over the edge so the camera feed on his helmet would capture the ship.

Intoh was silent for a long moment. "This has turned into something way bigger than we thought, so you hold there. Do not try anything until we assemble a bigger team. There is no question of infiltration without some serious backup now. The Verdant String Coalition will need to be involved in this."

Nick moved his gaze from Stru to Drake, saw the fury on his commander's face.

"Same as last time, then?" Drake asked Intoh. "Death by committee in the VSC?"

He heard Intoh's sharp intake of breath. "It's not the same as last time. This ship blew up the Cepi ruins. It's stolen Verdant String tech. This is a big deal, Commander."

"Last time was a big deal, too. Look how that turned out."

Intoh's voice rose a little. "I won't have you making unfair comparisons. I can't proceed without further advice, and you know it."

Drake didn't answer, and Nick felt like leaning over, ripping the comm unit off Stru's arm and throwing it down into the gorge below.

He didn't know about Drake, but he was not sitting around waiting for some VSC councilors to make a decision while Tila was down there, on her own.

Intoh let the silence tick by, and when she spoke again, her voice was a few degrees colder. "Stay put. We're sending the other teams to your position, and I'll contact SF Command for further orders."

She cut off the transmission, and Stru's worried gaze moved from Nick to Drake.

"What are you going to do?"

Drake moved closer to the edge to look over again and didn't answer.

"Bartega?" Stru sent Nick a desperate look.

"The thing is," Nick told him, "we don't take orders from Lieutenant Intoh, or anyone from Special Forces, for that matter."

Drake glanced at him over his shoulder, and there was a small smile on his face. "Yes. I don't think the lieutenant remembered that."

CHAPTER 18

NICK STARED at the black ship, which lay at the widest point in the canyon.

"It's a pity they aren't better pilots." Drake was looking at it with his helmet visor on zoom. "If they could have landed deeper into the canyon where the walls are closer, we could have landed on the roof and found a hatch or maintenance door in."

"They probably have sensors, though." Nick studied the way the ship was standing, a little off-kilter because a cluster of rocks to one side lifted it up higher on the left than the right. The struts had been deployed, but they weren't high enough to get it completely level.

"They've set it to dead mode, remember?" Drake said. "Sensors emit a signal. They won't have activated them. They're counting on the fact that there are too many places for them to hide on the Mother for us to even bother."

"Do you think the other teams have gotten here yet?" Nick looked right, toward where they had left Stru nearly an hour ago. Nothing moved, no lights were visible.

But this was Special Forces they were dealing with. They wouldn't see them coming until they were surrounded.

Nick knew if they'd stayed put as ordered, whether they were under Intoh's command or not, they would not have been allowed to do much more than protest from the sidelines.

Neither of them were prepared to accept that.

Stru hadn't liked them going, but he could hardly stop them by himself. He hadn't even tried.

They'd followed the edge of the cliff and ended up as close to the ship as they were going to get.

Which meant Intoh's team would be moving this way, too, as soon as they arrived. Nick's guess was that if they hadn't reached Stru yet, they would do so any minute.

"Something's happening." Drake tapped Nick's arm.

They both leaned a little further over the edge.

"Is that an all-terrain?" Nick watched as a bulky, windowless vehicle rolled down a lowered ramp, and drove silently off into the darkness.

"What are they up to?" Drake watched the vehicle until it disappeared.

"They're in dead mode, right?" Nick turned his head to look at Drake. "So they either have to switch their systems on to transmit a message, or they have to transmit from a mobile unit."

"They're communicating." Drake nodded. "They're either sending another message to the media on Parn, or they're talking to their friends."

"So, how about we hitch a ride back inside the ship when they come back?"

Drake set his pack beside him and pulled out his grapple. "Good idea."

They dropped from the top of the cliff face like earlings in a dive for prey, silent and fast.

All Nick could hear was the in and out of his own breath inside his enclosed helmet. Drake, rappelling beside him, didn't make a sound.

"Where are you?" Stru's hiss in his ear jolted him, and he had to breathe through the spike in his heart rate.

"Why?" He kept his voice soft and his tone curt.

"The first team is two minutes out." Stru's voice was unapologetic and equally curt.

The Special Forces officer was angry, no doubt about it.

His ass was on the line.

Nick's feet touched the gritty floor of the canyon.

"You are going to get killed or you're going to destroy any chance of getting the Halatian woman out." Stru's voice was low and uneven with fury.

"Is that so?" Nick knew they were taking a big risk, but he agreed with Drake that it wasn't as big as the risk they took by bowing to the Special Forces directives. "What do you think will happen here, Stru? The VSC will get involved. There'll be hand-wringing because Tila is Halatian. And while everyone weighs in, Tila could be whisked away. Right now, she's valuable to them. Most likely, if we're discovered, we're the ones who'll get hurt, not Tila. And in the worst case scenario, either they kill us, or they take us hostage too. Drake and I are prepared to accept that."

"Down comms." Drake's voice came through the comm in his helmet, but a brush on Nick's shoulder told him the commander was standing right beside him.

Nick wondered how long he'd been standing there in the gloom.

Damn, the man was quiet.

"We're going dark," Nick told Stru. "We'll contact you when we can."

"How long--?"

Nick cut him off and followed Drake, who was now just a dark shape ahead, deep in the canyon's shadow.

They would be impossible to see with the naked eye, and because they had managed to borrow full Special Forces gear, the smugglers would have difficulty with thermo-detection as well. Not that they were using it, if they were in dead mode.

Nick overtook Drake, moving a little faster than the commander as they navigated the twists and turns of the canyon.

They'd angled north along the top of the canyon and dropped down out of sight of the ship.

But they were closer now, and Nick started to move slower, to test every step he took before putting his foot down.

Somewhere ahead there was the sound of a scuff on the ground, and Nick crouched, signaling back to Drake to do the same.

A single guard trudged around the ship, shuffling in his thick boots and heavy suit. His helmet looked as if someone had scraped it against a rock.

Given the sleek, deadly look of the ship itself, the substandard kit was a surprise.

Everything they'd learned about the ship that had attacked Cepi was that whoever had built or stolen it had deep pockets.

The guard stood, looking in the direction the all-terrain had gone.

"He's waiting for them?" Nick wondered.

"If they've gone dark, they won't know when the all-terrain comes back. They've left someone outside with the codes to do a manual entry."

It made sense. It also made finding a good place to hide until the all-terrain returned more difficult.

They waited until the guard did another circuit of the ship, and ran as silently as possible to a small group of rocks when he was out of sight.

It was the best they could do.

Nick curled in on himself, and Drake pressed up against him. It seemed like a long time before they heard the crunch of the tires on the gritty canyon floor.

Thank goodness for the gravel or the all-terrain would have been past them before they even heard it; the pop and crack of stones under tires was the only sound it made.

As soon as it passed them, Nick rose up and ran, limping a little as the blood surged back into his numb feet.

Drake stumbled behind him, but righted himself in time, and they both swung up onto the backboard and then climbed up to lie flat on the roof.

The all-terrain slowed as it crawled up into the small loading bay.

The ramp lifted, smooth and silent, and Nick felt the pressure change as the enviro tech pumped air back into the chamber.

The guard who'd let them in pulled off his helmet, and after a moment, the doors at the back of the vehicle, and the driver's door at the front, opened.

"Well?" the guard asked.

"Zy managed to hack in to the pinch zone schedule, so we got what we needed, and she sent the message," the driver said. "But I need to speak to Jirmain. I think I saw a couple of personal hovers out there."

"Special Forces?" the guard asked.

"Who else?"

<h1 style="text-align:center">CHAPTER 19</h1>

SARTA WASN'T the only one who knew about the Mother and its significance to her.

But she was the most recent person Tila had told.

Hopefully it was fresh in Sarta's mind. Hopefully she'd pick up what Tila had been trying to say.

She'd told Commander Drake, too. In one of the comms she'd sent him when she was much, much younger. But the chances of him remembering that were very slim.

She'd told him a lot of things in those early years, her comms probably more open and personal because no one would let her speak to and see the real man.

She hadn't needed a filter, she was effectively writing to herself.

She'd outgrown it, mostly, by the time she was fifteen, although it carried on a little longer than that through force of habit.

It had come as a massive surprise to her when she'd left the support house at eighteen to go to university to discover that he'd been corresponding right back.

Actually, really, corresponding.

When she'd first been settled in the support house, she'd sent him little notes asking him and his wife questions, inviting them to lunch or dinner. She'd practiced tirelessly making his favorite things.

She'd never had a response. Had long given up expecting one.

Until a file entitled *Drake, Comms* had been flicked over to her handheld as part of her file.

She was so dumbfounded, so hurt, she hadn't spoken to Tui Jard since.

The comms had been kept from her for such dubious reasons, the mantra of 'for her own good' had worn so thin, she couldn't see how Tui could ever make amends.

She didn't honestly know if she had it in her to forgive.

Time would tell, although it had been over six years now, and she realized she still hadn't let it go.

Maybe it was time.

She remembered the roaring in her ears as Tui had flicked over the folder. Remembered the defensiveness on her house mother's face.

"I'd forgotten about them. It was only because I was collecting all your information to give to you that I came across them. We decided at the time that your attachment to Drake could only do you harm. He was a reminder of what happened, and he would never be able to live up to the expectations you seemed to have of him."

"Expectations?" She remembered the word was almost impossible to force out of her mouth.

"He'd rescued you. He was a father figure and a savior in one. In your head, he could do no wrong, but he was a normal man, and at the time, he was in particularly hot water because he'd disobeyed a direct order. Obviously he was rightly lauded for what he did, but there was still a technical process to go through. We . . . I . . . was afraid he wouldn't have the time to give you that you obviously wanted, so we decided rather than see you hurt, we would protect you from yourself."

"I see." She'd clutched her handheld in a tight grip, turned and walked out the door.

Tui had called after her, but she'd simply walked out to the street and called the next available EM, which had appeared within seconds.

She'd sent a friend to get the rest of her things.

Drake had read her comms, though, so it was just possible that Drake might understand her message if Sarta didn't. He'd asked her about where the smugglers hid while they were taking cover behind an air cooling unit on the *Caliope*. Special Forces had known the smugglers were using the Mother to go to ground, and she and Drake had talked about it a little while they huddled together.

She had sensed he wanted to leave her, to go back out and deal with whoever was shooting at them, but she had refused to let him go.

Not, she realized now, that he couldn't have pried her loose. She'd been ten, and half-starved. He'd been larger than life, and had carried her like she literally weighed nothing.

At the time, she hadn't thought of that, though. She'd felt able to hold him there with her will alone.

Too many people had been taken from her and she wasn't prepared to lose another. She'd held onto him for all she was worth.

He'd been resigned to it at first, and then he'd stopped trying to persuade her to let go after a while. He'd kept her with him, blocking her body, putting himself in front of her over and over again.

After his bravery, she still marveled that when it was over, it was touch and go as to whether he would come out of it with his career intact.

The cloud he'd had over his head made it all the more difficult to trust her new carers, her new people.

If she was so precious and valued, she'd wondered, why was the person who'd saved her in trouble for doing exactly that?

When he'd stepped down from his position in Special Forces, there had been such an outcry his commanders had to beg him to give a statement assuring the public he wasn't being forced out, that in fact they had offered him a promotion to stay.

He'd gone into the Protection Unit, and she'd hoped--it had been an unrealistic dream, she knew now--that he would have time to spend with her.

She was just one child he'd rescued amongst five hundred of them, and she could even see where Tui had perhaps been justified in thinking her expectations were too high when it came to Drake, but there had been no call to prevent her from reading the comms.

They had been everything she'd dreamed of.

She'd read them in her rooms at the university, and she'd tried to see them as she would have as a child. Tried to see if there was anything in what Tui had said, of his disappointing her, or not living up to her idea of him.

Maybe Tui hadn't read them herself. Maybe she'd had that much decency.

Even at eighteen, Tila thought his words were thoughtful and kind, and she wanted so much to go back to just after the rescue and start that conversation again.

She'd wondered at the time if she should send him a comm, letting him know that she'd just gotten his letters after all this time, but in the end, fear and shyness had the better of her.

She knew there was a chance he may not even remember her after so much time had passed, and the need she'd had for a relation-ship with a steady adult she trusted had come and gone.

She'd been an adult herself by then. Self-sufficient.

Perhaps that was what had hurt the most about Tui's betrayal. Tila's need for a trustworthy adult had been partly fulfilled by Tui herself.

It had taken time, but slowly, she'd given over her fear and her caution. She'd had to. She wasn't used to living in a state of anxiety, and so she'd given Tui her trust. And all that time, Tui had lied to her.

Tila scrubbed at her face.

Why was she thinking about this now? She'd put it behind her years ago.

Maybe it was meeting Nick. Then seeing Drake.

He hadn't forgotten her. He'd known her right away, she realized.

Said her name. There'd been recognition in his face.

Maybe she should have taken her courage in her hands and contacted him after all. Just to say thank you again, this time as an adult.

Next time she saw him, she would.

If she got out of this, if she kept going down the intriguing road Nick had invited her to walk, she'd get that chance easily enough.

It was almost funny. She'd skimmed along above the surface for so long, wary of putting her trust in anyone, and just when she'd made the decision to go deeper, she'd been yanked away.

Nick was down on Parn right now, probably worried about her.

She walked over to the window, hoping for a glimpse of her adopted home, but there was nothing but darkness. After a while she worked out that was because the window was in dead mode. There was no seeing through it. It was switched off.

Dun pinged the door and then walked in, and she turned from the window to face him.

"Why's the ship in dead mode?"

"So we're off the radar. Can't find something that's dead."

Of course. Of course they'd hide themselves from detection by going dead.

So even if her clue had been understood, whoever was out there looking for her still had to find the ship.

The Mother was big enough to make that an impossible task.

For a moment, she felt drained and absolutely done.

Then she forced herself to stand a little straighter.

At least she knew the score now. There would be no sitting around hoping someone would come. She'd done that on the *Caliope* and she'd lost hope long before Drake appeared to smash down the cell door and scoop her up.

This time, she'd have to make her own escape.

She crossed her arms over her chest and watched Dun walk toward her. "So, how many of the crew have worked out Jirmain's put a huge target on all your backs?"

Dun dropped the tray he was carrying onto the table. "I really should have let you be. Left you hiding wherever you were hiding."

"You really should have," she agreed. "No matter what happens, no one will forget about this. The deaths in the city, my abduction. You'll be hunted. And if they connect you to Cepi . . ."

Dun stared her down, and the door opened behind him. No ping, Tila noted.

Jirmain strode in.

"What's going on?" he asked Dun.

"She's warning of doom and gloom," Dun said, his eyes on her, not Jirmain. "Telling me the full force of Parn will be out for our blood."

Jirmain laughed. "I hope so."

Tila shook her head. "You're a smuggler. You've just reminded the Verdant String why they hunted smugglers down for years. And you've probably just revived the pastime."

He sneered at her. "They'd be doing me a favor if they revive the smuggler patrols. Less competition."

She saw Dun's reaction to his words, and moved to her left to keep Jirmain's attention on herself. "I thought you all supported each other?"

"I don't support the people who kept me as a slave. You see the trouble I've gone to to punish the people who sat around and 'discussed' what to do while I starved up on the *Caliope*? What do you think my plan is for the people who took me in the first place?"

"I'm guessing nothing good. But are the smugglers around today the same people who took you?"

"Not many, but some of them. And for others, it's a family business. The daughters and sons of the people who took me. You think I didn't think about what would happen when we blew up the Var Hub and Parn worked out it was smugglers?" He turned to Dun, but Dun's face was neutral again, the horror and loathing had been wiped from his face.

"Then my boy here," he hooked an arm around Dun's shoulders, hugged him close, "found you and brought you to me. And now we have the Verdant String thinking about evil smugglers again. There'll be a push to shut them down for good. I've managed to get revenge, revive the guilt in the Verdant String, and clear out the smugglers in one move." The smile he sent her was gleeful. He tightened his grip on Dun, then let him go.

"I want to leave soon." He turned to Dun. "There's a lot of traffic out toward the pinch zone, but Zy got into the traffic logs and it looks as if things will slow down in a few hours. We'll wait for a lull, and then pinch out to the black."

"If you have a safety pod, put me in it and drop me in a traffic lane." Tila leaned back against a wall. "You don't need me anymore."

"Oh, but I do." Jirmain gave her another smile, and this one was more sly than gleeful. "If I let you go, I'm giving them back something they don't deserve. I want them to tear at their hair and berate themselves for losing you. I want them to suffer, to be guilty all over again. They'll never know what happened to you, and it'll haunt them forever."

The look he sent her was chilling. He turned to Dun, and his expression changed from one moment to the other, serious and earnest. "Hine wants to speak to me about something important."

He strode out.

Dun watched him go, and kept looking at the closed door for a long time.

"You didn't know he was getting rid of the smugglers," she said.

He turned to her, eyes glittering, and then walked out himself.

She stared after him thoughtfully.

Jirmain might have got it just right in the way he'd played the people of Parn and the Verdant String, but he hadn't taken the reactions of his own crew into account.

Maybe he didn't care how they felt.

She had a feeling he soon would.

CHAPTER 20

THE CREW DIDN'T EVEN CLOSE the door between the loading bay and the rest of the ship behind them. The standard operating procedures of the VSC were obviously not adhered to in the smuggler community.

Nick waited until the sound of their footsteps faded, and then swung down from the all-terrain's roof. Drake landed lightly beside him.

"All we need is a system port. This is a modified VS652, so we should be able to get in." Drake walked to the door and flipped up a few covers Nick hadn't noticed.

"They said the ship that attacked Cepi was Verdant String tech, but I didn't know they'd narrowed it down to the exact model."

"Above your security clearance." Drake shot him an amused look. "And they only confirmed it two days ago."

Drake crouched down beside one of the open covers and pulled out his handheld screen.

"Why should it be compatible?" Nick stood beside him, keeping watch.

"Unless they've completely redesigned the system, why shouldn't it? And since our systems are pretty good, why would they? I'm sure the comms and the maps are encrypted, but the general ship systems should be accessible." He moved his screen close to the port and made a sound of satisfaction.

"It worked?" Nick risked a quick look down. Saw Drake had thrown up a three dimensional image of the ship above his screen. "They haven't got staff activation working, but given the lack of uniforms, that doesn't surprise me. So we can't tell where anyone is, but we can see where they're most likely to keep Tila."

Nick crouched beside him. "Do they have a brig?"

Drake pointed to it. It was only two doors down from where they were right now.

"Let's go."

He moved to the entrance, looked out and found the way clear.

When he got to the brig, he didn't need Drake to use his hand-held to get inside. Like the loading bay, the door was open and the one small cell was empty.

The sound of footsteps galvanized him to move. Drake ran back to the loading bay, and Nick ran after him. They took up position inside it on either side of the open door.

"You're saying you caught two hovers crossing up ahead of you on your scanner? But you're sure they didn't see you?" The man who spoke kept his tone calm.

"They kept going on their trajectory, and I stopped and waited to make sure they didn't turn our way before I came back."

"All right." There was a sound of a hand slapping a back. "We knew they'd be out there looking. It shouldn't be a surprise to catch them buzzing around. We're leaving as soon as the pinch zone clears a little, so don't worry about it."

"Sure, Jirmain." The man who spoke did not sound relaxed or calm. He sounded tense.

"Go take a break. You did well, Hine."

The all-terrain driver muttered something and then Nick heard him go.

The man he'd called Jirman stood silent for so long, Nick wondered what he could possibly be doing.

Then footsteps rang in sharp staccato past the open door and away.

Drake moved back to the system's port, and flicked up the ship's schematics again. "If she's not in the brig, she could be in the guest suite." He pointed to the room set between the captain and the navigator's rooms.

"That's if they're sticking to the VSC designations." The smugglers didn't have to adhere to standard VSC protocol. They might deliberately not stick to it.

Drake shrugged. "It's as good a guess as any."

True.

Nick took a last look at the plans and then moved to the entrance. The way was clear, and he worried about that.

Where was everyone?

Jirmain had gone left, toward the command center, and the all-terrain driver had gone right, to take the break Jirmain suggested.

The cabins were to the right, and it might be he and Drake had gotten lucky, and everyone was relaxing before they left for the pinch zone.

He moved forward quietly, but he stopped when a passage branched off to the right. A few doors down, in a closed room, he heard raised voices.

A number of people were very unhappy.

He turned to look at Drake, eyebrows raised.

The commander shrugged, then stepped past him and hunkered down in front of the door of the guest suite. It looked straight down the corridor where the argument was coming from.

The back of Nick's neck prickled at their exposed position, and he stood guard as Drake crouched beside the door, looking for a way to bypass the locks.

The raised voices down the passageway rose a little higher, and then cut off sharply, as if someone had turned a switch.

Then a door opened, and a man strode out, face set.

Dun.

Nick recognized him from the feed they'd gotten from the camera on Tila's dress.

The insurgent jerked back at the sight of Nick and Nick lifted his arm and shot him, keeping his laz on stun.

Drake turned at the sound, and a moment later, the door he'd been working on opened.

Nick ran forward, grabbed Dun's collar and then turned back, dragging him through the open door.

The room he stepped into was relatively comfortable, with a bed and a table and chairs. Tila Dor Rio stood in the middle of it, mouth agape.

The door shut behind them, and Drake moved to lock it.

Tila looked between them, speechless. "Special Forces?"

Nick frowned, and then remembered his helmet. He pulled it off.

"Nick?" Her voice was almost a squeak. She took a step toward him, hands together and reaching out, and he let go of his hold on Dun's jacket, dropping him to the floor and stepping over him. He pulled Tila close, running his hands up her arms and over her shoulders, to cup her face.

"Are you all right?"

She nodded, and tears glittered in her eyes. "I never thought . . ." She looked over his shoulder and gasped. "Commander Drake?"

She pulled out of Nick's hold and stepped toward the commander, again with hands outstretched. Drake reached out and awkwardly took her hands in his.

"I'm saying this now, before anything else happens. They only gave me your comms when I went to university."

Her words had an immediate effect on Drake. He tilted his head to one side.

"That . . . woman."

Tila nodded. "That woman."

She stepped back, releasing his hands as if suddenly shy. "I've wanted to say thank you for a long time. I told myself that if I managed to escape, I'd do it as soon as possible."

She turned to look at Nick, and gave him the sweetest smile. "And as it turns out, I didn't even have to escape to do it."

From the floor, Dun let out a groan.

She looked down at him, and frowned. "Stun?" she asked.

Nick gave a nod.

"I have to say, I'm surprised you found him outside my room. I thought he'd be off somewhere fomenting dissent." Tila worried her bottom lip with her teeth, in a way that was far too distracting.

"Dissent against who?" Drake asked.

"Jirmain, the captain."

Nick raised startled eyes to meet hers. "I think maybe you need to fill us in."

"The crew have worked out Jirmain has deliberately endangered them all." Tila felt a disconnect with her calm tone and the excitement and fear churning through her at having both Drake and Nick in the room with her.

They had risked everything to get her back, and she was very afraid Jirmain would have no compunction in killing them if he had the chance.

"Because his actions will revive the hunt for smugglers?" Drake asked.

She nodded. "He hoped for that outcome. He wants the smugglers chased down. What he forgot was his crew has links to the smuggler community, and they consider themselves smugglers still, whatever else they've become. Insurgents or agitators." She shrugged. "He may be able to walk away, but his crew can't or don't want to."

"So that's what the shouting was about," Nick said, glancing over at Drake.

"Shouting?"

"The crew were arguing their next moves, is my guess." Nick looked down at Dun with a considering expression. "He's coming out of it."

Dun's eyelids fluttered, and then they snapped open.

He looked up at Nick without any recognition, but when his gaze landed on Drake, he sat up. "You!"

"Me." Drake crouched down beside him. "You tried to kill me."

"Nothing personal." Dun slid back a little, putting a bit more space between Drake and himself. "Jirmain's orders."

Drake looked at him with focused dislike, and Dun turned his head to Tila.

"How about we make a deal?"

"Now, why would we do that, when Special Forces know exactly where you are, and have this ship surrounded?" Nick asked, voice soft and reasonable.

"Because even if they're out there, you're in here, and vulnerable. My way, no one gets hurt." Dun ignored Nick, and kept his gaze locked with hers. "I'm your best option. Jirmain will kill you rather than let you go."

"What form does this deal take?" Tila had a good idea, though.

"You let us go."

"I don't know that will be acceptable to the VSC." Drake rose back to his feet, towering over Dun.

"It will be if it means she gets away unharmed." Dun jerked his head toward Tila.

Nick and Drake said nothing in response.

Tila frowned. "Is that true?"

Nick seemed to have been working his way closer to her, because he was suddenly right beside her, gloved hand coming to rest on her back.

"Yes."

She shook her head, and her hair snagged on the pockets and straps of his suit. "But they killed so many people in Var. They shouldn't get away."

"This is a dead zone anyway." Drake's gaze fixed on Nick for a moment, then back to Dun. "We can't negotiate on VSC's behalf with you because we can't contact them to okay it. Help us get Tila out safely, and take your chances. At the very least, we'll all testify you did what you could."

Dun's lips thinned. "No. I'll get you two off this ship. You contact your people, get them to agree. We'll fly away, and tell you where to find Tila."

Nick barked out a laugh. "That's not going to happen. I'm afraid you're not exactly considered truthful. We leave this ship and let you go, we never see Tila again."

Dun shook his head in frustration. "Then what do you suggest?"

"I'm interested in that, too."

Everyone's gaze jerked to the doorway. The door had opened silently, and Jirmain took up the whole entrance, eyes dancing as if he was having a lot of fun.

He held a laz, and Tila noticed he'd pointed it very deliberately at her.

"My suggestion," she said, because no one else was speaking, "is that you let us take the all-terrain, and as soon as we're out, you try to run. You'd have the element of surprise, and Special Forces might take a few minutes to work out we're safe and still on the ground, giving you a little time to get away."

Jirmain might actually have a chance of pinching to the black if he got far enough from the Mother and had the space he needed. She hoped they didn't succeed. But they would have a chance, and everyone in the room knew it.

"Or I could just fly now, and all the same things apply," Jirmain said. "With the added bonus no one will shoot us down because they'll know you're onboard."

He'd barely gotten the last word out of his mouth when Nick shoved her back and stood in front of her.

Both he and Drake were shooting before she even understood what was happening.

The speed of it was shocking.

She had the impression of a coordinated effort, although she hadn't seen them communicating with each other.

Jirmain went down, his collapse silent and sudden.

Tila stared as Nick took two quick steps forward and crouched beside Jirmain, feeling for a pulse.

It was over. So quick and clean, it was shocking.

Dun suddenly struggled to his feet beside her, and as he rose she saw a flash, caught a glimpse of a laz in his hand, and then felt the still-warm end of it as he shoved it against her neck.

Drake toppled, going down with a sickening thud.

Tila made a sound, and tried to move forward, but Dun's arm was around her waist.

"No, no. You're not going anywhere."

Nick turned, his body angled so he could look out of the door and still keep an eye on Dun. "You had a laz the whole time?" His tone was bitter.

"I was on my way to take out Jirmain when you shot me." Dun gave a dry smile. He waved at Jirmain, still out cold on the floor. "Thanks for doing the job for me. And for keeping your helmets off so I had a headshot. Would have been a bit difficult to drop you in those suits, otherwise. Now, drop your laz."

Nick let it fall to the ground.

Enough of this. Just . . . enough.

"I need to see if the commander is alive." She jerked in Dun's hold.

"He should be, it's on the lowest setting." Dun tightened his grip. "Now here's what's going to happen, and it's good news all round.

"I don't have any attachment to you, Tila, except for the ticket out of here that you represent. So you'll be coming with me, and I'll keep the commander here, too, as a nice way to control you, seeing as you're so concerned about him.

"Soldier boy here can take Jirmain, put him in the all-terrain and drive off this ship. You can tell your friends in Special Forces they better let me go or Drake and Tila die. Then, when I'm at a safe distance, I'll dump Tila and the commander in a safety pod, and you can come get them. Everyone's happy. And you even have Jirmain in custody, as a nice bonus."

Tila could see the agony on Nick's face as he worked out there was going to be no way out of this.

"It's okay," she told him. "I think he will let us go."

"You'll have to trust me on this," Dun said, and she could hear the smirk in his tone. "You've got no choice but to do as I say."

Jirmain groaned from where he lay sprawled on the floor, and Dun casually moved the laz and shot him again.

"Get moving."

Nick reached down for Jirmain and started dragging him down the passage.

She and Dun followed, their movements awkward as he tried to keep her in step with him, his arm still around her neck. He choked her a few times before they got to the loading bay door.

"Drive the all-terrain around to the front of the ship. If I don't see you within ten minutes of closing this door, Drake dies. Fifteen minutes in, I start hurting Tila."

Nick didn't say anything, he simply dragged Jirmain to the all-terrain and opened the rear doors. "What are the codes?"

Dun called them out to him, and Nick heaved Jirmain up, threw him in the back, and then walked toward her, his gaze never leaving her face.

"Uh-uh. No further." Dun lifted the laz to her temple again.

Nick stopped, hands fisted at his sides. "I'm sorry, Tila. I should have done better."

Dun put a hand over her mouth. "Enough talking. Your time starts now, Soldier Boy. Get moving. And tell Special Forces I am deadly serious. You let us get away, or you'll be very sorry." Dun yanked her back and shoved her ahead of him. "Walk. I'm happy to shoot you and knock you out, or you can be a good little hostage."

He reached out an arm and slapped the door lock.

As it closed, Tila stopped and looked back, her gaze meeting Nick's.

"I'm sorry," he mouthed.

She reached out a hand, opened her mouth to tell him it wasn't his fault, that none of this was his responsibility, and Dun shoved her again.

As the door slammed shut, as she stumbled forward, she realized something.

Her anger was bigger than her fear.

CHAPTER 21

HE DIDN'T HAVE words for what he was.

Nick revved the all-terrain around the front of the ship, and tried to get a grip. Self-flagellation was not useful right now. He'd have plenty of time to beat himself up later.

He'd thought Dun was still mostly out if it. He definitely didn't think he had a weapon. Dun hadn't even tried to draw it when he saw Nick and was shot.

And the reason why he'd let all the fundamentals slip? He had been too focused on Tila, not enough on his surroundings, and because of that, he'd failed her.

He parked where the pilot should be able to see him, and the ship started to hum as Dun started it up.

Nick pulled on his helmet and flicked his comm on. "Lieutenant Intoh, are you there?"

"Bartega, you better have some good news." Intoh's voice was icy.

"I have the mastermind of the Cepi disaster and the attack on Var, but Drake and Tila are still in the ship, and the new captain says he wants safe passage off the Mother, and he'll leave both of them in a safety pod when he's at a safe distance."

There was silence. Nick didn't make the mistake of thinking the lieutenant had dropped out. She was just trying to rein in her temper, most likely.

"And where are you, Sergeant?"

"In an all-terrain vehicle from the ship. The person who is behind all of this doesn't have a suit, so it was the only option when I got him out."

"We see you." Intoh's voice leveled out a little. "What's the story, Bartega? Who've you got with you?"

"A Halatian called Jirmain." He heard Intoh's quick intake of breath. "As he made Tila say in her forced statement earlier, he was taken by smugglers when Parn Special Forces overran the *Caliope*, and he was kept by them.

"He seems to have fought his way up, and has made some friends with deep pockets, but his mistake was setting the VSC back on the smuggler community.

"The other smugglers didn't like it," Intoh guessed.

"When the rest of his crew realized they and their friends in other smuggler ships would become targets all over again, there was a little coup onboard."

"And now someone else is in charge." Intoh sounded intrigued.

"The new leader is Dun, the man who carried out Jirmain's orders in Var, blowing up the buildings."

Intoh swore. "So not reasonable, then."

Nick hesitated. "He has a lot to lose if he's caught, which is why I believe him when he says he'll kill Drake and seriously hurt Tila if we don't follow his demands. But he also isn't the fanatic about the Halatians that Jirmain was, and I think he will drop Tila and Drake off when he can."

Intoh was silent for a moment. "All right, that's good. Or better than nothing. It doesn't look like we have much choice, anyway. No way is Special Forces going to move against him and risk Drake and Tila. No possible way." She sighed. "Tell him we'll let him leave, and move that all-terrain back."

Nick flicked the comms on the panel in front of him on. "Dun."

"Yes, Soldier Boy? Good news, I hope?"

"They'll let you go without shooting. I'll move the all-terrain back, and then you can take off."

"That works."

Nick closed his eyes in frustration. "I better have Tila and Drake back safe in a couple of hours."

"Or what?" Dun asked him, almost in a whisper. Then he laughed. "Don't worry, I've got no need for either of them. I'll toss them back at you."

He better.

Nick reversed the all-terrain and then sat and watched as the ship rose up into the air in a billow of moon dust.

He better, or Nick would hunt him to the ends of the galaxy.

Drake opened his eyes and blinked them rapidly.

"You're all right." Tila leaned against the edge of the bed, hovering over him, but his eyes didn't focus on her face. "Dun shot you in the head with a laz, but he said the setting was low."

"I can't see." His voice only had a slight hitch as he turned at the sound of her voice.

Tila swallowed hard. "You can't see?" She crouched beside him, hands shaking.

"It's common for a head shot." Drake patted her arm, and she realized *he* was comforting *her*.

"How long does it take for your sight to come back?" She gripped his hand and squeezed it.

He hesitated.

"It does come back?" Her voice was faint.

"In a couple of hours, or sometimes, surgery is required."

Med tech could fix most things. Including sight. Drake wouldn't be blind for life if there was more permanent damage. But it didn't mean he wasn't going to have a hard time.

And all because that bastard Dun had taken her. "I should have changed my hair years ago." The words burst out of her, raw and painful.

"What? Why?" He patted her arm again.

"Because it's blue! That's the only reason Dun took me. If I'd stripped the color from it--"

"No." Drake's tone was fierce. "You should be allowed to be yourself."

"I'm afraid that's not working out so well, Commander."

They were both silent for a long moment. Eventually, Drake struggled to sit up.

"Tila, what's happening? Where is Bartega?"

Tila forced herself to focus. "Dun shot you, put the laz to my head, and used the leverage of that to force Nick to take Jirmain off the ship in the all-terrain and negotiate with Special Forces on his behalf. The deal is they let the ship go, and he drops us off in a safety pod when he's a safe distance away."

"Will he, though?"

She nodded, then realized he couldn't see her. "I think so. He isn't like Jirmain. He isn't interested in a new Halatian motherland."

Drake stilled. "That was Jirmain's end game?"

"It sounded like it was a fantasy, not something he'd thought through enough to ever actually accomplish." She took his hand in both her own again. "But he's down on the Mother with Nick, so we're dealing with a different dynamic now."

"Where's my laz?" Drake's voice dropped to a whisper.

"I don't know." She twisted around, looked carefully where Drake had fallen, but there was nothing. "I can't see it."

"It's okay, I'd have been astonished if they hadn't got it. It's useless to me, anyway, but you . . . can you shoot one?"

"I've never even held one," she admitted.

He withdrew his hand from hers and started patting down his

leg, pulled a tab on his pants, and drew a slim, small laz from the pocket.

"It's a mini-laz. They aren't as powerful as the standard weapon, but they're easier to hide." He held it easily, even though he couldn't see, and ran his fingers along the bottom. "See this slide?"

"Yes." Her whisper was hoarse.

"You slide it to the right, and the laz is activated. You push this," he gently ran his finger over a button, "and it shoots. Simple aim and fire, Tila. It's easy."

"All right." She took it, slid it into the pocket of her jacket. "But it may do more harm than good. I'll have to choose wisely, because if I let this play out, I think he will let us go."

"Agreed." Drake sounded reluctant, but he nodded. "If it looks like he's going to renege on the agreement, you've got nothing to lose, though."

"That's true." She'd have to be very sure before she attacked him. Very, very sure.

"I thought about you often over the years." Drake changed the subject suddenly, dropping his head back down on the pillow. "I wondered how you were getting on."

"I wondered about you, too. I came so close to contacting you when Tui gave me the comms you'd sent, but then I talked myself out of it. I thought you would hardly remember me."

"How could I do that?" he asked. "It was one of the most memorable days of my life."

She slid down to the floor, leaning back against the bed, and tilted her head so it rested near his. "I learned to bake marsalos, because they were your favorite."

He was silent for a long time, so long, she thought he might have passed out again, and she started to turn to check on him.

"My wife, Kay, and I, would love to come visit you when this is over," he said. "And I can try them."

"That's sounds like a deal, Commander." She closed her eyes and smiled. "Although, you might have to fight the Marsalos Fiend for your fair share."

"You mean Bartega?" Drake's voice was derisive. "*He'll* have to fight *me*."

She laughed, and that's how Dun found her when he stepped into the room.

"Glad you're having fun." His expression was tight. "You're needed on the pilot's deck. Both of you."

Turned out, they really were needed on the pilot's deck.

A woman with a severe, no-nonsense expression, and smooth, dark hair pulled back from her face, wasn't going to let Dun go far without proof that she and Drake were okay.

"Here they are." Dun flicked his hand in their direction, his full attention on the screen and the woman.

Tila was holding Drake's arm, guiding him as he walked surprisingly well for someone who couldn't see. She met the woman's eyes, and all she could see in them was annoyance.

Well, she supposed this was a big headache for Parn Special Forces.

"You don't look too well, Commander." The woman's voice was even more clipped when she spoke to Drake.

"Blinded by a laz hit," he said, his own voice mild. "Otherwise fine."

Her lips thinned, and then she took a deep, deep breath and looked straight at Dun.

"All right, you can make your way to the pinch zone." Her words were less stiff, as if she'd accepted her new reality and was dealing with it. "We'll talk again there."

"No! Wait--"

She cut the comm, and Dun stared at a blank screen.

"We're going to die." Someone stood to Tila's right, and she realized there were three seats tucked up against the bulkhead. She turned a little to see more clearly, and came face to face with the thin, almost waif-like woman from the comms room who had given her such filthy looks earlier.

"We're not going to die, Zy." The snap in Dun's voice switched Zy's focus from Tila to him.

"Yes, we are. And you and Jirmain will have killed us."

A few others stood from their seats, as well, and Tila counted at least six people.

"We don't have time for this." Dun turned away from her, pointed to another crew member. "Rina, navigate to the pinch zone. If it's clear, we pinch out."

"It won't be clear," Zy scoffed. "They'll have that place ringed with big ships, so we won't have the space to pinch out. We'll be trapped."

"We have the Halatian and Drake, we're not without bargaining power." Dun turned back to her.

"Not without bargaining power for Special Forces," Zy conceded. "But nicely pinned down for anyone who wants to take out the whole ship so none of us can talk. Who do you think Jirmain was dealing with, the Benevolent Society?"

Dun froze. "You think they'll attack us in the pinch zone?"

"Was Cepi too long ago for you to remember?" Zy's voice was bitter. "Yes, they'll attack us."

"But Jirmain was the one who attacked the base on Cepi," the navigator Dun had called Rina spoke up.

"On whose orders do you think?" Zy asked. "Do you think he wanted to wipe out his Halatian treasures? No, he did not." She sent another vicious look at Tila.

"You arranged the comms, heard what they said to him?" Dun asked her.

She nodded. "They were insistent. No hint or rumor was to get out about them. They are very afraid the VSC will launch a full-scale attack on them if they have even the flimsiest of proof."

"The Breakaways," Drake said. "The Breakaways are involved."

"Of course they are." Zy's voice rose. "Who else has the land available to offer Jirmain a motherland? It's one thing for the VSC to guess the Breakaways are involved; but this ship has comms and files in its system that point right to them. And the people concerned aren't going to let us pinch out to the black with what we have on them."

There was silence on the deck.

"Jirmain gets away with it again," Dun said bitterly. "He's nice and safe down there--"

"How long do you think for?" Zy openly jeered. "How long did the Arkhanian councilors and moles who helped us on Cepi last before they mysteriously died? I'd give him five minutes."

A cold chill ran down Tila's arms and her breath caught. She hoped Nick had turned Jirmain over by now, that he wasn't near enough to him to be caught up in any crossfire.

"Turn yourselves in." Drake's voice, calm and deliberate, cut through the rising panic. "What have you got to lose?"

"I've got a lot to lose." Dun stared around the room, and then focused on a spot behind her shoulder.

Tila glanced back, saw Kirt and Timbo in the doorway.

"The three of us have got a lot to lose, because we bombed those buildings in Var."

"Take a safety pod, and go," Drake said. "Let the rest of the crew hand themselves over."

"We'd still have the same problem as Jirmain. We won't last long, no matter where we're kept. They don't know how much we know, so they'll tie off all the loose ends, just to make sure." Zy crossed her arms over her chest. "Giving ourselves up to Special Forces will just put us in a place where we can't escape, so they can get to us more easily."

"Then what do you suggest, Zy?" Kirt's tone was sarcastic. "All I'm hearing is what we can't do."

She sent him a look that should have scorched him where he

stood. "We run. We don't pinch out here. We run and we pinch out somewhere else. We go now." The urgency in her voice affected everyone present.

Tila could sense the tension, could sense the landscape changing. Dun would have let her and Drake go. Zy was a different story.

Tila didn't know Zy's objectives, but the power structure had shifted from Dun to her. That was clear.

"If you're going to run, then let us go." She stepped closer to Drake and looked around at the crew, appealing to everyone. "Drop us out in a safety pod. The VSC search for you will be a lot less focused if we're safe and they have Jirmain. Take us, and they won't stop looking."

There was a moment of silence.

"She's right." Kirt stepped deeper into the room. "If we drop them in a pod and they tag Special Forces, that would be the best time for us to make a getaway, while everyone is scrambling to get them back."

There were nods around the room.

Tila held her breath.

"Let's do it." Dun said at the same time Zy gave a reluctant nod.

They stared at each other, and Tila wondered if their power struggle would take place in the open. But Dun eventually looked toward Kirt without saying anything.

"Take them to a pod and then let me know the moment you eject it." He turned to Rina. "As soon as I give the word, we go full speed."

"In which direction?"

Dun glanced at Zy, but when she kept quiet, he faced Rina. "Any direction that's away from the pinch zone."

Everyone seemed to relax a little now there was a plan in place.

Kirt caught Tila's eye and jerked his head toward the door. "Let's go."

"So far, so good," Tila murmured to Drake as she steered him out the room.

"That was quick thinking." Approval rumbled through his voice. "But keep that gift I gave you ready, just in case."

Kirt's stride was long and he was in a hurry, so when they caught up with him, he was visibly seething at the delay, giving an impatient wave to get them through the door into the safety hatch.

She had to bite her lip to stop herself saying something to him. They had grabbed her, put both her and Drake into this situation, and now they couldn't wait to be rid of them.

If hurrying wasn't also in her own best interests, she would have delayed him on purpose.

Instead, in silent rebuke at his attitude, Tila solicitously helped Drake through into the room.

Kirt didn't apologize, but he kept his mouth closed as he pulled down a safety pod, clamped to an extendable metal arm, and opened it up for them to climb in.

"I've set the comms to general, so you can make an open call for help."

Drake paused, half in and half out of the pod.

"What?" Kirt's voice was impatient.

"Nothing." Drake lifted his other leg, and Tila helped him into his seat and clipped him in. It wasn't nothing--Drake didn't hesitate for no good reason--but they'd have plenty of privacy soon to talk about what was bothering him.

She climbed in herself, and as she was clipping in, Kirt reached up to grab the transparent lid and pull it down.

Before he lowered it, though, Zy stepped into the room, and he turned to her, face relaxed, eyebrows raised in question.

"Message from Dun?"

"I'm not Dun's lackey." Zy shifted, as if she found it difficult to keep still.

Tila put her hand in her pocket and closed it over her mini-laz.

"Well, what then? You're slowing things down here, when you were the one bleating about how we're all going to die." Kirt took a step toward her, and she lifted up a laz.

"Yes, we're in a rush, but this won't take long."

Kirt lifted both hands. "What the hell, Zy?"

"If she kills either Commander Drake or me," Tila said into the silence, "the VSC will never stop hunting you."

Kirt glanced over at her, gave a reluctant nod. "That's true."

"True for you, because you were caught on camera in Var." Zy's lip curled derisively. "They don't know who I am or that I even exist."

"They'll find out." Kirt was looking at her with more and more dislike. "How long do you think it will take the smuggler community to start talking to the VSC once they find out why they're being persecuted again? How long before a list of the crew Jirmain assembled gets handed over?"

Zy hesitated. Shrugged. "So, they find out. This will still be worth it."

"What, exactly, do you plan to do?" Tila asked.

"A little bit of insurance." Zy kept the laz on Kirt, but she was looking at Drake and Tila. "Commander Drake here left Jirmain on the *Caliope*. He looked him in the eye and left him."

Tila sensed Drake tensing beside her.

"I was on the *Caliope* myself. And I can tell you that it was chaos. And the only people to blame for what happened to Jirmain were the people who captured him in the first place, and the people who abducted him a second time and took him away."

"My people, in other words?" Zy sneered.

"Your people," Tila agreed. "That's why Jirmain included crushing them as part of his plan."

"And yet, he also blamed Drake." Zy's arm moved, and she pointed her laz at the commander.

Tila squeezed his arm, hoping he would realize he was in the line of fire.

"Zy, what's it to you? Jirmain's battles aren't ours to fight." Kirt's expression was careful, like he was talking to a child.

She turned to him, face contorted in rage. "He's dead. Dun killed him by putting him into Special Forces hands. I can do this one thing for him before we go. And besides," she wiped away a tear, "as I say, it's insurance. Jirmain's backers wanted the commander here dead. It was a bonus, Jirmain said, getting paid to kill someone he'd have killed for free. If they do catch up with us, that's one ace we'll have up our sleeve, that we carried out their bidding, even when we didn't have to."

"Why do they want me dead?" Drake asked.

Zy started, as if surprised her victim could talk. "I don't know. I don't care."

"No idea at all?" Drake asked, and Tila waited, just in case she had some information.

"No." Zy's answer was short.

Oh, well. If she didn't know anything . . . Tila lifted her arm and shot her straight on, and watched her collapse on the floor.

"I hope I won't have to do the same to you," she said politely to Kirt, turning the laz on him. "But if you close the lid, we'll be happy to leave."

Drake made a sound, as if he was holding back a laugh.

"Is she--?" Kirt looked from Tila to Zy, sprawled on the floor.

"Just unconscious."

Kirt nodded, lowered the lid, locked it, and swung the arm to the nearest chute. Then he tapped his comm.

Telling Dun they were about to eject, she guessed.

They dropped suddenly into free fall.

She caught a glimpse of the black of space, the far-off glow of the Mother, and then it seemed as if they were grabbed by a giant hand and thrown, tumbling end over end, while blinded by light.

Drake cried out.

"Explosion," she managed to get out as her world spun. "The ship--"

She looked back, and as the rotation of the pod slowed down, she saw that where once had been a ship, now there was nothing.

CHAPTER 22

DEBRIS PELTED THE SAFETY POD, each crack and thud loud enough to make Tila think it would breach the hull.

"Turn on the nav system, let's see if we can power out of here." Drake patted the console almost exactly where the nav system was located.

Tila stretched across and activated it, and a strange, grinding sound filled the cabin.

She hit the deactivation button and stared at the console as it lit up with various warning lights.

"Debris in the thrusters." Drake's voice was disgusted. "This model was recalled and destroyed twenty years ago for that very reason."

"My guess is some of the snatch barons setting up the Breakaways got their hands on them before they were destroyed." A big piece of debris hit them, hard enough to spin them in a new direction, and her last word squeaked out.

"Is there anyone out there?" Drake had set his seat upright, even though he was still blind, and he strained against the harness keeping him in place, as if he wanted to explode out of his chair.

She angled her neck so she could look up as well as straight out of the transparent lid of the pod, but there was nothing to see but parts of Jirmain's ship.

"No."

Of course, if something was directly behind them, she'd never know it.

"You think we're asking for trouble, using the comms?" She looked over at Drake, and saw he had relaxed a little back into his seat.

"That's why I hesitated, back on the ship when I was getting into the pod. They were worried about Jirmain's backers shooting them down. Using an open comm would have meant the backers could hear us, just as well as Special Forces."

"Only, they weren't shot down. They were blown up." It couldn't have been a laser strike. No laser strike could completely destroy a ship in a single hit. Which meant there had been an explosive hidden onboard which had been detonated.

"Agreed." Drake rubbed his eyes. "It was either detonated remotely, through a bug sitting in their system, or . . ."

"Or?"

"They got close enough and activated the bomb using a signal."

"With Special Forces converging on the pinch zone?" She looked out again, but there was nothing but the ruined pieces of a space ship.

"That's why they did it now, before Dun got to the pinch zone." Drake rubbed at his eyes impatiently. "I remember that moment, you know. That Jirmain described to Zy."

"You really saw him on the *Caliope*? What happened?" She never thought for a moment Drake would have deliberately left him there.

"I was under fire. I was carrying you, and he seemed safe enough. He was in a cell, like the one I'd taken you out of, and I thought that was probably the safest place for him until the fighting died down."

"That makes sense. It's just . . . when you're in a cell, anywhere else seems better." She could see how Jirmain had built his anger over the years. "He wanted out, and then he was trapped there and couldn't get away when the smugglers took him again."

Drake sighed. "I went back, found the cell empty. I thought one of my team had gotten him out. I didn't see him again, but that wasn't surprising. I was more or less under arrest after that, until all charges were dropped."

"It's not your fault. I meant what I said to Zy. The fault lies with the smugglers."

"And with the Verdant String Council. Everything the smugglers did could have been prevented if the Coalition had acted in time."

"Yes." There was nothing more to say to that. She either let it go, or it ate away at her forever. Amends--as much as were possible--had been made.

A piece of debris knocked against the pod with a thud, and sent it into another slow roll.

As they turned, she thought she caught a glimpse of a ship.

"I think--" She drew in a sharp breath as they rolled again. "I think I saw a ship." She'd caught the glow of the Mother off a wing, more than anything.

"VSC?" Drake demanded.

"I wouldn't know the difference, I'm afraid. But yes, it looks sort of like the ships on the broadcasts."

Drake grunted. "It's coming closer?"

"I can't see it anymore, and surely if it was a Special Forces ship, it would be making contact?"

"Then send out a call," Drake's voice was grim. "Our reason for not using the comms was to stay hidden. If they've found us, we might as well make as much noise as we can, and hope Special Forces is listening."

***

"We have a signal."

The comms tech looked up, eyes wide with relief.

It was the first words spoken since they'd all seen something flicker just beyond the curve of the Mother, and Intoh had ordered the pilot to move as fast as she could.

"Who from?" Nick felt his heart squeeze tight in his chest.

He realized he wasn't breathing, and forced some air into his lungs.

"It's Tila Dor Rio. She says she's in a safety pod with Commander Drake, and that the ship they were on is--" The comms tech stopped talking abruptly as they rounded the Mother and the first pieces of debris hit the ship. "Gone." He finished his sentence in a whisper as the pilot pulled them to a halt.

"Who is that?" Intoh leaned forward, looking at the nav screen, which showed another ship.

Nick dragged his gaze away from the nav and up to the massive transparent wall screen that took up the whole front of the pilot's deck. There in front of them, looming silent and massive behind the tiny yellow safety pod, was another VSC ship.

"One of ours?" Tyr, Intoh's second-in-command, asked.

"If so, why aren't they saying hello?" Intoh brought up a screen on her chair and typed something in. "Are you seeing this?" she said.

"I am." The voice was deep, and one Nick thought he recognized, but he didn't have time to place it. Tila was right in front of him.

Right there.

Why was she staying where she was? "Why aren't they using the inboard thrusters to head toward us?"

"She says the thrusters are jammed."

"Let me go out in a small tow and fetch them." Nick turned to Intoh. "Right now. Let me go."

She cocked her head. "Do you not see the big, mysterious ship hanging there, Sergeant Bartega?"

"I see it." He held her gaze.

"They are most likely not friendly." Tyr crossed massive arms over his chest.

"We caught them by surprise," Nick said. "They wondering if they shoot the safety pod, will we shoot them?"

"And you think this because . . .?" Intoh raised her brows.

"Because why else are they still here? They've got a VSC ship which they clearly shouldn't have. My guess is that while they do have a ship, they might have less powerful weapons, maybe even non-standard weapons, because while it may be possible to steal the parts to make a ship, I imagine it's a lot harder to steal the parts that make a laser cannon."

"Hmm." Intoh nodded. "And if I let you got out there, what do you think will happen?"

"Hopefully, I'll rescue Tila and Drake." That's all he really cared about.

Intoh blinked, as if she was expecting a more tactical response. "And if they do decide to try their luck and fire?"

"Then they do." Nick wasn't going to sit here waiting for a what-if.

Intoh turned to Tyr. "Get Bartega into a tow."

Nick gave her a nod of thanks and jogged off the deck, Tyr right behind him.

That ship wasn't going to sit there forever. At some point they would have to make a decision. Nick would rather disrupt their plans sooner rather than later.

CHAPTER 23

"WHAT'S HAPPENING?" It was the second time in five minutes Drake had asked the question, and Tila detected the edge of his cool beginning to unravel.

He wasn't used to being unable to direct things.

"Nothing. Special Forces went quiet when they saw the other ship, and they haven't transmitted since."

"That's wise, since we're on an open channel. Whatever they say to us, they say to whoever's in that ship."

"I just wish--" She stopped, frowning as a small vessel dropped from underneath the Special Forces ship and started toward them.

"What?" Drake reached out a hand and gripped her arm.

"Special Forces are sending a little . . . pod toward us." She tried to make out exactly what it was.

"A tow, maybe?" Drake put his hands over his eyes in frustration.

"Maybe."

Another piece of debris hit them, and she couldn't help jumping. The sound reverberated through the pod, and she had to steady her breathing. "Just more debris," she said as calmly as she could.

The mystery ship started moving forward, so slowly she didn't notice it at first. It was more like they were drifting than engaging their engines, but before the tow came out, they had definitely been stationary.

"I think the other side is reacting to the tow. Moving closer."

"They're hoping to intimidate Intoh into withdrawing." Drake shook his shoulders, as if trying to release tension. "Is it working? Is Intoh backing off?"

"No. The tow is still coming."

Something was building here, a stand-off with the safety pod in the middle.

"Why aren't the strangers running?" she wondered. "Special Forces must have called for reinforcements by now. They must have."

"Whoever blew up Jirmain's ship is wondering if we know anything about them, wondering what Dun and Jirmain might have let slip. And weighing up the risk of killing us versus getting away as fast as possible."

"They're taking their time about it." Tila knew she sounded grumpy. She *was* grumpy.

Drake snorted out a laugh. "It's obviously a big decision for them. And my guess is they're also conferring with someone who isn't onboard. Someone who's calling the shots. They won't want their signals intercepted, so they're routing the comms through multiple filters. I'm betting they're waiting on instructions, and they don't know what to do about the tow. Intoh was smart to move so quickly, it's probably left them scrambling."

"I wonder if Nick is onboard?" She hadn't meant to mention Nick, but he was right there, at the forefront of her thoughts, the tip of her tongue.

"What's the story with you and Bartega?" Drake's tone was a little gruff.

"We're neighbors," Tila said. No way was she saying anything else. What may or may not happen between her and Nick was too new, too uncertain, to say out loud.

"The tow?" Drake asked as a smaller piece of debris hit them.

"No, but it's close." She couldn't see who was piloting it, but whoever they were, they'd extended a mechanical arm from somewhere in the front, and the next bang on the pod's outer casing was the arm clamping on.

"Here we go." Tila moved her gaze reluctantly from the tow and its clamp, and turned to the mystery ship.

It moved in a sudden spurt of speed, shooting forward and sitting directly above the safety pod.

From where she half-lay, half-sat in the pod, she could look up through the transparent lid and stare at the underside of the ship.

"What is it?" Drake's voice rose.

She was breathing in short, panicked bursts, and she swallowed, made herself take a deep breath. "They sort of lunged forward, and they're right above us, now. Like a predator defending its kill."

The safety pod jerked and then began to move, and Tila watched the underneath of the mystery ship slide away as the tow pulled them out.

"It hasn't stopped the tow. They're taking us with them." She twisted in her seat, looking back at the ship to see what its response would be, but it stayed where it was as the tow moved steadily back, drawing them closer and closer to the Special Forces ship.

"We're nearly there." She was still having trouble with her breath, waiting for the other side to decide to shoot them, but just as they reached the safety of the launch bay, the mystery ship spun around and shot away, disappearing almost in the blink of an eye.

"They're gone," she whispered. "They pinched out."

"My guess is, they still hadn't gotten word on what to do, and Intoh's backup is coming. They had to know shooting us would be risking their lives, and maybe they weren't prepared to make that call without an explicit order." Drake relaxed back in his seat.

"Whoever piloted that tow has steady nerves and courage to spare." She didn't know how they had kept going with the ship looming over them.

The pod thumped down on the launch bay floor, and the door

sealed behind them. She watched the lights go from orange to blue, signaling the air was now breathable.

A figure dropped out of the tow, and then a face appeared right beside her, looking in.

Nick.

He would be getting all the marsalos he wanted.

CHAPTER 24

"THERE WAS A SECOND ATTACK ON JIRMAIN." Nick leaned back in Tila's armchair and rested his ankle on his knee.

"Unsuccessful?" Tila sipped at her jah.

"Yes. He still won't talk, which I can't understand. As soon as he does, they have no reason to kill him anymore."

"Or they promised they'd kill him more painfully if he talks than if he doesn't," Tila speculated.

Nick glanced over at her, gave a slow nod. "Maybe."

"I see you and the commander are all over the screen." She didn't like it, but she tried to keep the unhappiness out of her voice.

"You are, too." Nick was watching her with a steady gaze.

That was true, but unlike Nick and Drake, she wasn't obliged to give interviews. Her picture though, a still taken from footage of her being dragged through the streets of Var by Dun, as well as one taken as she walked out of the space port to an EM with Nick and Drake when they got back to Parn, was getting a lot of play. The victim and the heroes.

It would seem her life was on some sort of repeat.

"It'll die down."

She tipped her head from side to side, unconvinced. "Eventually. But maybe if I'm not around I'll speed that along."

"Oh?" He became very careful.

"I've had an invitation to visit Arkhora."

Nick frowned. "Who do you know on Arkhora?"

"No one. Nyha Bartali has invited me, and Special Forces has offered me passage. Nyha was caught up in what happened on Cepi, and it will be good to talk to her. To go somewhere else for a bit and get out of the public eye."

The foot balancing on his knee dropped down, and he leaned forward. "When?"

"When can you get leave?" she asked him. "That is, if you want to come?"

He drew in a deep, quick breath and stood in a fluid move. Put out his hand, and when she took it, drew her up into an embrace.

"I thought you were saying goodbye, or some crazy thing like that."

"Now why would I do that?" she whispered into his ear. "Just when I'm getting used to the tension."

EXCERPT: BREAKAWAY

CHAPTER 1

LEO GAUDIER WALKED A DANGEROUS PATH.

Sofie didn't pretend that wasn't part of what attracted her to him in the first place. She was all for sticking it to the Core Corporations. All for it with bells on.

And it didn't hurt that she'd really liked the look of him since they'd met.

There'd been a little catch in her heart, a little hitch in her breath. A trembling, like fear or excitement. She'd never been affected like that before.

And it didn't hurt that he'd been interested right back.

Well, generally men all seemed interested, all did a little chasing, but she wasn't into hooking up with some guy in an Upper Reaches bar.

That wasn't in her plan. She'd just been there to eavesdrop on loose-lipped Cores employees.

Until Leo.

Leo Gaudier was the first one she hadn't actively run from too fast for him to catch her.

She'd run a little, but it was more out of habit.

He'd been just tenacious enough, but not obnoxious with it.

If she'd said no, it would have been no.

No matter how fast he made her heart beat, she'd never have taken the next step with him if it had been any other way.

Now she sat watching him on their third dinner out together with almost embarrassing stars in her eyes, even though the dangerous stuff he was into had just reared its head and interrupted their evening.

Because it was part of the package, and she'd already acknowledged she liked everything she saw when it came to Leo, she didn't show so much as a flicker of displeasure when his comm sounded and he'd stood and excused himself from the table.

It wasn't as if she was all that unencumbered herself. He just didn't know it yet.

They were halfway through an excellent dinner at the best restaurant on Felicitos, the ground-tethered way station on the planet Garmen, otherwise known as Breakaway 1.

The views were spectacular.

From where she sat, up against the window, Sofie could see the curve of Garmen below, the blue of the ocean glimmering far in the distance as the last of the evening light touched it.

Higher up, in the levels of Felicitos that edged out beyond Garmen's atmosphere, it was harder to see the details of the green, blue and rose planet.

Prices and rents went up the lower you got, and you couldn't get any lower than The High Flyer.

She seldom saw this view. She couldn't afford it. But sometimes, like now, when she did see the aching beauty of the curve of the planet, the breath-stealing vistas, she grudgingly conceded her father's work did mean something.

Not everything--she'd never give him that. But it wasn't for nothing, either.

Sofie turned away from the sights and looked over at Leo again.

He stood at ease, hands in pockets, his back to her, talking into his comm a little distance from the other diners, in a small alcove designed specifically for privacy.

He had removed his jacket--it was hanging over the back of the chair opposite her--and he stood in a perfectly fitted shirt and trousers, quite delectable from his dark, slightly wavy hair, broad shoulders and down over long, lean legs.

Sofie lifted her glass of truly excellent wine, turning the glass this way and that to admire the almost luminous lavender hue of it, put it to her lips and took a sip. She shifted in her chair and caught the very last of the setting sun on the planet below her.

A movement caught her eye, a reflection in the glass of the window, and she tilted her head to better see what it was.

A man stepped out of the service entrance, which wasn't strange-- waiters had been coming and going since they'd arrived--but there was something in the way he moved.

Years of survival, of assuming danger was all around her, snapped her spine straight.

It took an effort of will to force herself out of the fear, out of the frozen helplessness that descended for the split second it took for the man to walk from the service door to halfway across the restaurant floor.

She was getting complacent. She had things cushier now than she ever had, and it was dulling her edge, she realized. A lapse like that, a victim's paralysis, would have seen her with her throat slit and her body lying in an alleyway faster than she could snap her fingers in the old days.

But she was back to her old self now, the shock of an attack in this cocooned pocket of luxury over with.

She almost smiled at herself. Nowhere was truly safe, and she'd been lying to herself if she thought otherwise.

She moved her head a fraction, looked at the man under the sweep of her eyelashes.

He was making for Leo.

There was no rush about him, nothing to indicate he meant harm, but she never ignored her intuition.

Never.

Leo's bodyguard, who was sitting three tables away, had his eyes on his boss, not on the waiter, and Sofie knew calling out to warn Leo wouldn't work.

The assassin would just shoot that much faster.

Instead, she knocked the nearly empty bottle of lavender wine into Leo's almost full glass, then exclaimed loudly and jumped to her feet, brushing at her clothes, although she'd made sure not a drop of it landed on her pale gold evening dress.

Damned if she would ruin it.

She bent, one hand on the table for balance, as she slipped off her high-heeled gold sandal, and saw Leo had started to turn.

The assassin had, too; eyeing her for a second before dismissing her outright, and focusing back on Leo.

Leo's bodyguard, Zan, flicked his gaze in her direction, and something in the way his eyes jumped over the assassin had her radar screaming high alert.

Inside job.

No doubt about it.

She lifted her shoe and threw, aiming for the assassin's hand as it came out of his pocket with a tiny laz.

The sharp heel tip caught his fingers, and he dropped the slim weapon with a cry more of surprise than pain.

Leo was looking at her by now, eyes wide, and they widened even more when she picked up the fallen bottle of wine and threw it at his bodyguard.

By the time it had smacked Zan in the chest, Sofie saw Leo had pulled a laz of his own.

The assassin dived for his weapon and Leo shot him.

It happened fast, but Zan was still in play--she saw his arm rising up, laz in hand, aimed not at the downed assassin but at Leo.

She'd already tugged off her other shoe and she ran at the bulky guard, screaming to distract him.

He started, flinching as she came at him, shoe raised over her head, and although he got a shot off at Leo, it wasn't the head shot he'd clearly been aiming for.

Leo went down, but his hand went to his chest.

Sofie threw the shoe, then scooped up the fallen bottle of wine while Zan stood, arms raised for another shot at Leo, and swung it at his head.

Hard.

He crumpled.

For the first time, she became aware of the other diners.

Couples were looking at her with eyes wide, mouths open.

She turned away from them, picked up her shoes, which had conveniently landed near each other, and hopped into them one at a time as she headed for Leo.

"Can you stand?" She kept her voice low.

"Just about." His words were strained and his breath labored.

"You're wearing an anti-laz layer?"

He shook his head.

"Ouch." She put an arm around him and hauled him up with his cooperation.

When he got to his feet and could stand without her, she looked quickly around, picked up his comm unit which lay on the floor near the window, and then scooped up his jacket from the back of the chair and her own little bag.

A faint whine and the whiff of ozone had her turning in fright, but it was Leo, laz in hand, pointed in Zan's direction.

She didn't know if he'd killed the bodyguard or just made sure he stayed unconscious.

She didn't want to know.

The restaurant staff had disappeared the moment trouble started, something she was sure wasn't lost on a number of the patrons, but now a wild-eyed manager stumbled out of the same door as the assassin.

Sofie didn't know if he were trying to extract payment or let them know the meal had been on the house--she didn't give him a chance to say anything.

With all their belongings under one arm, she slid her other under Leo's shoulder and half-dragged, half-supported him to the door.

The manager made a sound at the back of his throat, and she sent him a hard glare, shutting him down, and then staggered out with her burdens through the lavender frosted doors.

CHAPTER 2

SOFIE ERDO WAS NOT who he thought she was.

Leo leaned against the wall of the lift, breathing through the pain, and watched her as she bent over her screen, face fierce with concentration.

He belatedly remembered this was the Lower Reaches, and she would need a code to operate the private lifts, but she obviously had one. He didn't have the energy to ask her how.

"Do you have ports?" she suddenly asked, looking up at him.

He nodded, slid a shaking hand into his pocket and handed the portable money credits over to her. She took them without a word and went back to her screen.

He tried to work out exactly what had happened back in The High Flyer.

His thoughts kept catching on her elegantly leaning over the table, one foot in the air behind her, as she reached back and took off a delicate golden shoe.

Then she'd thrown it, and all notions of delicacy had disappeared. Lethal seemed the best description to replace it.

She'd looked lethal.

The thug the Cores had sent after him hadn't expected to be hit by the sharp heel of a shoe, and Leo had almost lost the advantage she'd given him because he hadn't expected it, either.

And then there was Zan.

The bastard had been with him nearly a year.

He wondered what they'd done to get to him, but depressingly, they'd probably just offered him money.

That was the way of things on the Breakaways.

The sole reason for the two planets' existence.

Zan had been part of his security team when they foiled the last attempt to get him two weeks ago. It was why Leo trusted him to work solo tonight, but the Cores were obviously getting desperate enough to part with large amounts of money to end this stalemate.

They'd already killed two of his people this month.

Leo wondered what they'd managed to get out of them before they died.

The bodies had been dumped outside his warehouse, just to make sure he understood how much they'd suffered before they'd been murdered.

And as a warning to his other staff.

Resist talking, and you won't go easy.

He felt a sudden lightness, as if he could float upward, and wondered if it was the laz hit, or if he really was almost weightless as the lift plummeted down. It decelerated suddenly, and the lift door pivoted open.

Sofie stepped close to him, put an arm around him and took his weight.

She drew him out of the enclosed space as fast as she could without hurting him more, and that, more than anything else, quelled the tiny voice in his head that said this might be a set-up, that she might be part of the Cores' plot.

He'd tried to entice her into revealing her stance on the Cores before, and she'd kept her opinions bland and disinterested.

The woman who'd foiled an assassination attempt with two

sandals and an empty bottle of wine didn't have a bland bone in her very lovely body.

He wondered how she planned to get them out.

While Leo knew the powerful owners of the Cores had originally mandated a single entry and exit point when they built their tethered way station, that had proved so impractical, they'd had to create several.

What they had planned to be a tightly controlled structure was in fact a leaky sieve. Still, if they were behind this attempt to murder him then they'd be watching all of the ways out.

Sofie gently pushed him up against a cold stone wall and then tap tap tapped away on her heels, taking her warmth and the truly lovely scent he couldn't get enough of with her.

The stone told him they'd gone deep. Underground deep.

Every part of the way station that sat above the ground was tough, rigid and as light as the engineers could get it. It was only the underground levels that would include stone.

He'd never come down this far.

He didn't even realize the lifts reached this low and that anyone other than authorized personnel would have the codes to get to it.

One thing he was sure about, Sofie Erdo was not authorized personnel.

There was a faint squeak of rubber wheels on a smooth surface, and then Sofie was back.

He forced eyes he hadn't realized were closed back open, and saw she'd gone to fetch a tiny electro-magnetic cart.

"In you go." She got an arm around him, and he staggered toward it. As she lowered him down, she lost her grip on him, and he fell awkwardly into the passenger seat.

Pain overwhelmed him.

When he struggled back to consciousness, he guessed only a moment or two had passed because they were still in the same spot, but Sofie was stroking his face.

There were tears on her cheeks, which made him frown. She

gave an exclamation of relief when she saw he was back, and ran around to the other seat with the tap tap tap of her shoes, and eased the EM off into the darkness.

"Where . . . going?" he mumbled. He didn't hear her answer.

Panic gripped him, spiking his adrenaline and bringing him a little more into consciousness.

"It's all right." Sofie glanced at him. "I'm getting us out of here."

Her words shouldn't have calmed him--he'd just come to the conclusion he didn't know her at all--but they did. He leaned back in his seat, and let the darkness around them swallow him up.

Leo was a big man.

Sofie looked down at him and considered her options.

Picking him up was way beyond her. She guessed his weight was nearly double her own, and while she wasn't short by any means, he was a good head and shoulders taller than her.

She didn't want a repeat of what happened near the lifts. She'd seen him go white with pain as he hit the center console between the seats of the EM with his injured side and then pass out.

It had shaken her, and she'd try just about anything to make sure it didn't happen again.

She'd have to engage brain power here, rather than muscles.

She looked around her at what she had to work with.

The EM track ended in front of what appeared to be a solid wall in a narrow passageway. On one side, an air pump hummed quietly, and lightweight metal boxes lined the opposite wall, labeled with the names of spare parts.

The wall wasn't a dead end, though.

She went to the air pump and typed a code into the keypad on its lock mechanism.

There was a faint click, and the end wall popped open, swinging outward on its hinges.

The EM wouldn't work beyond this point, though, an oversight so egregious she felt like chasing down a few of the construction workers who'd created it and yelling at them.

Of course, they'd built it in secret, risking their lives to create hidden ways into the tethered way station the Cores didn't know about. And this wasn't the only one they'd built.

But still.

You needed to be able to walk out for it to be useful. And Leo wasn't walking anywhere right now.

She opened the door wider, peering down the tunnel to see if anyone had left anything useful inside for her.

There was a hand-pulled hover cart.

She stepped in and walked over to it. To her relief, when she switched it on it started smoothly and lifted up on its cushion of air. It looked big enough to take Leo from head to waist, but nothing else.

The cart suggested someone was using the tunnel to bring goods out or in, but whatever it was, they weren't taking or delivering large quantities.

She wondered who it was. She'd have to thank them, because the cart was a lifesaver.

Stretchy ropes with hooks lay beside it, to secure whatever was piled onto the cart's tray. She sighed. This wasn't going to be fun, for either of them.

Sometimes, she knew, life wasn't fun. It only made the times that were all the more enjoyable.

She turned back to the EM cart and Leo. He looked vulnerable, so unlike she'd seen him before, when he was all cool control.

Tonight had not gone as planned, for either of them.

She wondered with a little spike of worry if there had been anyone in the restaurant who could identify her.

There were scanners watching what happened in Felicitos, but she'd heard a rumor that that wasn't true of the exclusive restaurants frequented by the top echelon of the Cores. They didn't live in a do unto others spirit. With luck, no one would want to admit to seeing anything, either.

It was the safest way to go on Garmen.

She shrugged the worry off. Nothing she could do about it right now, and she had bigger problems on her hands.

She took a deep breath, straightened her shoulders and leaned in to the cart, getting an arm around Leo, bracing herself, and levering him up.

He came up a little way, and fell back down.

His eyes fluttered open.

"You have to help me, Leo." She was panting with effort. "Come on, up you get. Just a few steps, I promise."

He seemed to hear her, struggled up, and it was enough to get him on his feet, leaning heavily on her.

Once they were both upright, she was seriously worried he would take them both down.

"While I like all the muscles, believe me, they are very problematic right now." She couldn't move more than a few shuffles at a time.

By the time they'd reached the hand cart, she was sweating, and close to collapse.

She felt a deep sense of dismay when she tried to work out how to lower him down without hurting him.

Eventually she threw his jacket on the cart where she thought his head would land, and bent, then knelt, grabbing at him as he slid down. He hit the cart, but not as hard as he could have, lying across it at an angle.

It was the best she could do.

She stood, catching her breath and stretching out the kinks in her back, then pulled the wall closed behind her.

She could have sent the EM cart off, but if the system was working, it would go where it was needed as soon as someone on this level hailed one, and if it were discovered in this strange place, the location would be put down to the bugs in the system.

From everything she'd heard, there were a lot of bugs in the system.

She gave a wicked grin, then turned back to the cart and Leo, and steeled herself for some hard work.

She maneuvered him, pulling his legs around to get him straight, and used the stretchy ropes to create a sling over her neck and shoulders to hold his legs off the ground on either side of her body.

The cart moved better if she was in front, pulling it, and she'd gotten about halfway down the tunnel when she heard him make a sound. She turned to look at him over her shoulder.

He was blinking up at her, bemused.

"Am I dreaming this?"

She shook her head. "I'm afraid not."

"How embarrassing," he murmured and then closed his eyes again.

She smiled. Turned back and carried on pulling the cart.

It seemed like he would live.

ALSO BY MICHELLE DIENER

SCIENCE FICTION NOVELS

Verdant String series:

Interference & Insurgency (Two Novellas of the Verdant String: Box set)

Breakaway

Breakeven

Trailblazer

High Flyer

Sky Raiders series:

Sky Raiders

Calling the Change

Shadow Warrior

Class 5 series:

Dark Horse

Dark Deeds

Dark Minds

Dark Matters

HISTORICAL FICTION NOVELS

Susanna Horenbout and John Parker series:

In a Treacherous Court

Keeper of the King's Secrets

In Defense of the Queen

Regency London series:

The Emperor's Conspiracy

Banquet of Lies

A Dangerous Madness

Other historical novels:

Daughter of the Sky

FANTASY NOVELS BY MICHELLE DIENER

Mistress of the Wind

The Dark Forest series:

The Golden Apple

The Silver Pear

SHORT PARANORMAL FICTION

Breaking Out: Part I (Short story)

Breaking Out: Part II (Novella)

To receive notification when Michelle Diener's next book is released, you can sign up to her new release notification list.

ABOUT THE AUTHOR

Michelle Diener is an award winning author of historical fiction, science fiction and fantasy.

Michelle was born in London, grew up in South Africa and currently lives in Australia with her husband and children.

You can contact Michelle through her website or sign up to receive notification when she has a new book out on her New Release Notification page.

Connect with Michelle
www.michellediener.com

facebook.com/michelle.diener.author

twitter.com/michellediener

instagram.com/michelle_diener_author

bookbub.com/authors/michelle-diener

amazon.com/author/michellediener

goodreads.com/michellediener